BY JANET EVANOVICH

ONE FOR THE MONEY	TO THE NINES
TWO FOR THE DOUGH	TEN BIG ONES
THREE TO GET DEADLY	ELEVEN ON TOP
FOUR TO SCORE	TWELVE SHARP
HIGH FIVE	LEAN MEAN THIRTEEN
HOT SIX	FEARLESS FOURTEEN
SEVEN UP	FINGER LICKIN' FIFTEEN
HARD EIGHT	SIZZLING SIXTEEN

VISIONS OF SUGAR PLUMS
PLUM LOVIN'
PLUM LUCKY
PLUM SPOOKY

WICKED APPETITE

FULL HOUSE

WITH DORIEN KELLY

LOVE IN A NUTSHELL	THE HUSBAND LIST

WITH CHARLOTTE HUGHES

FULL TILT	FULL BLOOM
FULL SPEED	FULL SCOOP
FULL BLAST	

WITH LEANNE BANKS

HOT STUFF

WITH INA YALOF

HOW I WRITE

AVAILABLE FROM HARPERCOLLINS

HERO AT LARGE
MOTOR MOUTH
METRO GIRL

FULL SPEED

JANET EVANOVICH

AND CHARLOTTE HUGHES

St. Martin's Paperbacks

This is a work of fiction. All of the characters, organizations, and events portrayed in this novel are either products of the author's imagination or are used fictitiously.

FULL SPEED

Copyright © 2003 by Evanovich, Inc.

For information address St. Martin's Press, 175 Fifth Avenue, New York, NY 10010.

ISBN: 978-1-250-04075-6

Printed in the United States of America

St. Martin's Paperbacks edition / September 2003

St. Martin's Paperbacks are published by St. Martin's Press, 175 Fifth Avenue, New York, NY 10010.

20   19   18   17   16   15   14   13   12   11

PROLOGUE

JAMIE SWIFT PACED THE PARKING LOT OF Hank's Pump-n-Pay as she tried to decide her next move. She was mad enough to chew a barbed-wire fence, and her anger had a name to it: Max Holt.

Jamie needed help. She needed someone to talk to, and she needed a ride.

She spied the phone booth and hurried toward it. Who to call? It was after midnight. People with any kind of sense were usually home in bed at this hour. She had to calm down. She sucked in three deep breaths and was immediately hit with a wave of dizziness. She grasped the metal counter beneath the telephone. It would be her luck to hyperventilate right here in the parking lot, fall on her face, and be scarred for life. Yeesh.

Jamie spied the sticker on the pay telephone that read: *DESPERATE FOR HELP?* CALL LEND-A-HAND *HOTLINE*. She leaned closer and read the small print: *We're Here for You Twenty-four Hours a Day.*

Desperate, the advertisement read. That was her, all right. Desperate with a capital *D*. Plus, she was losing her mind. Or what was left of it after two weeks of dodging bullets from a drive-by shooting, almost getting blown to smithereens by a car bomb, and falling into a river and into the path of a hungry alligator. Hell's bells, she was lucky to be alive.

Jamie plunked two quarters into the pay phone. Her hand trembled. The fact it had started raining didn't even faze her. After what she'd been through, that was small potatoes.

Big potatoes was being stranded in a Podunk town she'd never heard of in the middle of the night, with her best friend more than two hours away. Big potatoes was being ogled by a gas station attendant whose oil-stained T-shirt stretched tight across a belly that had obviously sucked down a record number of Budweisers. She glanced his way. Even from a distance he looked dumb as cow dung. Probably had a tattoo on his butt that read *This Side Down* just in case he forgot. He looked at her like he hadn't seen a woman since inside plumbing. Like the kind of man people wouldn't let near their barnyard animals.

She dialed the number.

"Lend-a-Hand Hotline, this is Tanisha."

"Oh, thank God," Jamie said, glad to hear another voice. "I'm, uh—" She glanced down at the ad once more. "I'm desperate."

"Could you hold, please?"

There was a click. Jamie blinked. And waited. She would not cry. She was made of tougher stuff than that. Tough as nails, that's what she was. She glanced toward the man inside the gas station, not more than fifty feet away. Yeah, he really did look kind of goofy. Like maybe there were a couple of orangutans hanging from his family tree. Like maybe his parents had been first cousins. Jamie stared right back at him. Finally, he looked away.

"Hello?" The woman named Tanisha was back.

"Yes. My name is Jamie, and I'm in trouble."

"Are you pregnant and scared and suffering feelings of isolation and helplessness? Afraid of telling your parents?"

Jamie blinked. "No."

"Are you depressed?"

"Well, I—"

"Are you having trouble sleeping at night or sleeping too much? Experiencing appetite changes, feelings of sadness or doom, unable to get up in the morning?" The woman paused, drew in breath, and went on in rapid-fire succession. "Have you lost interest in people, places, or things that used to bring you pleasure? Do you enjoy sex?"

"Sex?"

Huge sigh. "Girl, you got to work with me, 'cause I've got a possible jumper on the other line and I'm the only one working the phones tonight."

"I've never done this sort of thing before," Jamie confessed.

"Me, neither. It's my first night."

Jamie slapped her open palm against her forehead. A rookie.

"Listen up. Does your problem have something to do with a *man*?" Tanisha said the word as though it weren't fit to be used in polite company. "'Cause I know about men, honey."

"Sort of."

"Sister, you hold right there while I try to talk this idiot off the roof of his house. If he don't get off this time, I'm going over there personally and push the SOB."

Another click. Jamie wondered if she'd made a mistake by calling. Maybe she wasn't as desperate as she thought; she certainly hadn't considered diving off a rooftop. That had to be a good sign. The man in the gas station had settled down with a magazine, and the rain had slacked off. Things were looking up.

Tanisha picked up. "OK, I'm all ears."

". . . AND SO THERE I WAS, RUNNING MY LIT-tle newspaper in Beaumont, South Carolina, minding my own business. . . ." Jamie paused. "Did I tell you that I own the newspaper? My daddy left it to me when he died. It has been in my family for years."

Silence.

"Hello? Tanisha? Are you there?"

The woman on the other end yawned. "Do you think we could cut to the chase, Jamie? I don't need your life history, and to tell you the truth, my attention span isn't that great. I think I have ADHD."

"Oh." Jamie realized she *had* been talking for some time, but she'd assumed Tanisha would need background information if she was going to help. "OK, so the next thing I knew, this gazillionaire, Maximillian Holt, blew into my life like a bad wind and turned it upside down. See, I need balance and predictability. Max is not a predictable person."

"So what's the problem? Were you born without feet so that you couldn't walk away?"

"It wasn't as simple as that," Jamie replied. "Max is my silent partner. He kept my newspaper from going bankrupt."

"OK, so this is a business problem."

"No." Jamie glanced toward the gas station. The man inside was sleeping, head thrown back, slack-jawed. Maybe he was harmless after all. She went back to her conversation. "Max and I were a team. Not only were we trying to investigate corruption in my town, somebody hired a couple of hit men to kill Max. And guess who found herself right in the middle of it? The gunfire shattered the windows at my newspaper office. If Max hadn't pushed me down on the floor, I wouldn't be talking to you right now."

"Wait a minute, what's with this hit men stuff?" Tanisha asked.

"We think this big-time preacher from Sweet Pea, Tennessee, ordered the hit. He has mob connections. He wanted to buy Max's TV network, but he couldn't scrape the money together fast enough. When Max sold it to another person, someone was mad enough to hire a hit."

"Girl, what'choo mean coming to me with hit men shit? Am I going to lose my kneecaps for hearing this?"

"Nobody knows I called you."

"Listen to me," Tanisha said. "This is police business. I'm going to hang up now."

"Hey, I put fifty cents into the phone. Don't I get some advice? Plus, I was hoping you could tell me where I could get a ride."

"I am not being paid enough to handle mob-related problems. I have a family: a husband, three kids, six brothers, and two sisters. I have cousins, aunts and uncles, grandparents. I have three cats and a beagle. I've got more relatives than the Brady Bunch and the Waltons put together. I can't just disappear into one of those witness protection programs, you get my drift?" The woman on the other end of the line gave a huge sigh. "Just answer me this: Where is Max now?"

"He dumped me."

"Excuse me!"

"We were on our way to Tennessee, you

know, to go look for this minister and his mob friends. Max waited until we got two hours out of Beaumont, and he just stopped the car in the middle of the road and turned around. Said he was taking me home. Said I would, quote, just be in the way, unquote." She paused. "After all we'd been through together, I lost my temper. I made him stop the car. We had this huge fight on the side of the road, and, well . . ." Jamie paused as she recalled their argument. "It was bad."

"So what did you do?"

"Fortunately, it happened close to a gas station, so I walked over."

"And he just drove off and left you?"

"Actually, he came back for me, but I refused to get in." Jamie paused. "Maybe I overreacted."

"You think?"

"I'm better off without him, Tanisha. All I've ever wanted was to live a normal life. Max is not normal."

"Girl, there ain't no such thing as normal."

Jamie thought of Phillip, the man she'd almost married because he'd seemed so safe and normal. Yet his mother had been the ringleader of the corruption in Beaumont. "You may have something there, Tanisha."

"And you don't want to go nosin' around some crazy preacher with mob friends. Besides, it sounds like you and Max are done."

Jamie didn't answer.

"Hello?"

"It wasn't all about Max," Jamie said. "I was hoping to land a story for my newspaper. I could just taste the headlines, Tanisha: *Renowned Evangelist Hires Hit Men to Take Out Millionaire Tycoon.* This story could have given me my big break. Not only would it have sold newspapers, it probably would have been picked up by the Associated Press. I'll bet *Newsweek* or *Time* magazine would have bought it. This is the kind of story I have always wanted to write."

"Look, you asked for my advice and I gave it to you."

"You're saying I should walk away from my big story and let Max have the final say?" She was suddenly indignant. "I don't *think so*. I have always made my own decisions."

"Hey, it's not like I'm charging you for this, you know. You want to end up buried beneath a concrete building, go for it." She sniffed as though she were truly peeved. "Besides, I think you had your mind all made up long before you called me."

Jamie stood there for a moment, letting the words sink in. "You're right, Tanisha. I just needed to talk it out. To hell with Max. I'm going to Sweet Pea, Tennessee, whether he likes it or not. Besides, I got something he doesn't have."

"And that would be?"

"I'm a woman, that's what. And from the information we've already gotten on the man, it seems this preacher likes women. They're his weakness. I'm going to bait him, Tanisha. I'll have him eating out of my hand so fast he won't know what hit him, and when I get finished I'll have the story of my life."

"What about Max?"

"What about him?" Jamie hung up, a satisfied smile on her face.

ONE

JAMIE'S EXCITEMENT ABOUT GOING TO TENnessee was short-lived. How the heck was she going to get there without a car? Her vintage Mustang was in the shop back in Beaumont, South Carolina: dented, banged up, with a couple of bullet holes.

She needed a plan.

She needed wheels.

The rain started to fall once more. What she really needed at the moment was either a really big umbrella or a place to stay for the night.

Jamie glanced at the sign on the road that read: *Whittville: 2 Miles.* That didn't tell her much; she'd never heard of the town.

She watched a tow truck turn in to the gas station and pull up beside one of the gas pumps. A big man in navy overalls climbed out and began pumping gas. He glanced at her, politely tipped his cap, and nodded, as though it were an everyday occurrence to find a woman pacing the parking lot of a run-down gas station at this hour.

Hmm. Maybe he could give her a ride.

Jamie approached him. He looked harmless enough. He was middle-aged and wore a wedding ring. His overalls were snug; he looked well fed. Probably had a wife at home who spent a lot of time in the kitchen. They probably ate their dinner on those cute little folding tray tables in front of the TV set while sitting in matching recliners. Their relationship was probably simple and uncomplicated.

The man caught her staring. "Good evening, ma'am."

The name Buford Noll had been stitched on a little patch sewn to his overalls. Yep, he looked respectable enough.

"Good evening to you, Mr. Noll," Jamie said, trying to sound upbeat. "I was wondering if you could give me a lift into town. I'll pay you."

"Well, sure. Any place in particular?"

"I need to find a nice, inexpensive motel for the night."

"Oh, well." He rubbed his jaw. "The one in

Whittville is pretty run-down. Probably have to go all the way into Jessup."

"How far is that?"

"'Bout twelve miles."

"Like I said, I'll pay you."

"Oh, you don't have to do that. I'm headed that way, but I got to make a quick stop first."

Jamie was relieved. "Thank you."

"You can go ahead and climb on in, Miss . . ."

"Just call me Jamie." She hurried around to the passenger's side. Things were definitely beginning to look up.

PARKED IN THE SHADOWS ACROSS THE STREET, Max Holt watched Jamie climb into the tow truck. She had not seen him return; she had been talking on the telephone.

"What's she doing now?" a voice asked from the dashboard.

"Looks like she just found a ride home."

"Man, you really screwed up big-time."

Max stared at the blinking lights on the front of the dash. A former NASA scientist had designed his car, a Porsche look-alike, only bigger, with a virtually indestructible titanium exterior. The car held state-of-the-art equipment, which ranged from a global positioning satellite system to a full videoconferencing suite and a high-powered computer that ran it all. Max had personally created artificial intelligence with voice recognition technology that would not be available for years to come.

His invention, which he called Muffin, had a Marilyn Monroe voice and "she" could literally think for herself. Muffin was stubborn and mouthy and, as ludicrous as it sounded, capable of emotion. She was constantly taking in data, but unlike other computers, she formed opinions and made judgment calls. And thanks to his sister, Deedee, who was in the throes of menopause and had complained to Muffin of her symptoms, Muffin had processed the information and was now suffering the same malady.

Muffin, too, was going through menopause. She had hot flashes, mood swings, and she threatened to shut down her own hard drive permanently each time Max crossed her. Currently she was having an on-again-off-again on-line romance with a laptop computer at MIT. She was almost more than Max could handle. To say that he had created a monster was an understatement.

"What are you going to do now, big shot?"

Muffin asked. "Mr. Love-'em-and-leave-'em?" she added, never one to mince words.

"That's not the way it was between Jamie and me."

"Yeah, and that's what really has you pissed. I mean, who would have thought it? There's actually a woman out there who doesn't think you're the best thing since on-line trading."

Max tightened his grip on the steering wheel as he watched the tow truck pull away from the parking lot.

"I was trying to protect her. This job is going to be dangerous. The good Reverend Harlan Rawlins and his mob pals are probably looking for me as we speak."

"But that's not what you told her, was it? You told her she would only get in your way."

"That's how you deal with a woman like Jamie. If I had told her I was afraid for her she wouldn't have listened."

"So you decided to hurt her feelings instead. Great idea, Max. You shouldn't have agreed to let her come in the first place."

"You're the one who insisted I bring her."

"You never listen to me. Besides, I wouldn't have advised you to do it had I known you would dump her halfway to Tennessee."

"It's better this way," Max said. "I need to

think clearly, and I can't do it if Jamie's around."

"Look, I don't have time to take on your personal problems, OK? My job is to keep you out of trouble and make you look good by providing you with any and all information you might need."

"Thank you."

"You still screwed up."

Max shook his head as he started his engine and put the car into gear. It shot off, leaving a dust cloud in its wake.

TEN MINUTES AFTER JAMIE HAD CLIMBED INTO the tow truck, she found herself on a dirt road in a remote area. The truck's headlights provided the only light. "How much farther?" she asked.

"We should be coming up on it soon," Buford said. "We're looking for a pink-and-white house trailer with a brand-new SUV parked in front of it."

The shabby-looking mobile home appeared right after the next bend. A white Ford Explorer was parked out front. "Nice wheels," she said. "Looks like it just rolled off the showroom floor. Don't tell me the owner is already having mechanical problems."

Buford grunted. "The new owner is having problems making payments. That's where I come in." He turned into the driveway.

"What do you mean?"

"It's being repossessed. I'm here to pick it up. Thank goodness there are no lights on, that means he's asleep. Makes my job a whole lot easier." He put the truck into reverse and backed toward the SUV.

Jamie gaped. "You're taking this person's car?"

"He hasn't made a payment in three months. I'm just doing my job." He put the truck into neutral, set the emergency brake, left the motor running. "Better lock your door. Some people don't cotton to having their vehicles towed off like this."

"Wait a minute," Jamie said. "You said you had to make a quick stop. To me a quick stop is hitting a McDonald's drive-through window or maybe grabbing a cup of coffee to go at the Waffle House. You never mentioned repo'ing somebody's vehicle."

"Won't take me long," Buford said, climbing from the truck.

"Oh, no." Jamie twisted around in her seat

and watched Buford unwind a cable and attach a massive hook to the underside of the SUV. He hit a switch, and a motor churned to life. The vehicle climbed upward.

Suddenly a light flashed on inside the trailer. Jamie scrambled across the seat and leaned out the driver's window. "Someone's up," she said.

Buford glanced toward the mobile home. "Oh, shit."

Suddenly the trailer door was flung open and Jamie caught the silhouette of a man holding a shotgun. He fired into the air. Jamie ducked. Buford dived beneath the truck.

"Get away from my car!" the man shouted.

"You done missed three payments, mister!" Buford called out loudly. "I've been hired to tow it in! You cause trouble and I'm calling the cops!"

The man fired again. A bullet pinged off the side of Buford's truck. "Holy hell!" Jamie cried, and hit the floor.

"Stay down!" Buford told her. "They're always upset at first."

Jamie closed her eyes. It was happening all over again. For some reason that she couldn't fathom, people insisted on shooting at her.

"What are we supposed to do in the mean-time?" she replied loudly.

Buford didn't hesitate. "I reckon we wait."

THE SMELL OF FRESHLY CUT LUMBER GREETED Max as he stepped inside the cabin with his bag. No surprise there; the cabin had been renovated and redecorated for his use. Even so, the construction crew had kept the antique heart pine floors intact, knowing that Max, who was personally doing renovations to his home in Virginia, would appreciate them. The furniture was simple; probably much of it had already been in place. Max was grateful for that as well. The fact that he could afford to build a brand-new cabin with all new furniture and appliances did not mean he preferred it. Simplicity and comfort was more his style.

As usual, his staff had taken care of everything from securing the place to providing groceries. Max looked inside the refrigerator and cabinets and nodded his approval. His people knew his likes and dislikes, right down to the brand of beer and cold cuts he preferred. He checked out the two bedrooms and decided on the loft area. He spent an hour on his cell phone, finalizing his plans. He and Muffin had worked tirelessly once they'd gotten back on the road, but Max was a man who left nothing to chance. He knew what he was facing, knew the dangers.

By morning he would have all the information he needed on Harlan Rawlins, celebrity evangelist. Max hoped Muffin would be able to get information on Harlan's mob connections as well. Max's plan was simple: First, find Rawlins. The hit man who'd tried to kill Max had been linked to Rawlins, and Rawlins was supposedly linked to the mob.

Rawlins and his mob friends obviously felt they had a score to settle with Max because they'd lost the bid on his TV network. It would have been the perfect vehicle for Rawlins to spread his word and draw in literally hundreds of thousands of new members. New members meant more money, and owning a TV network would have made the mob more powerful than ever. It was no surprise they were angry; the only question was, how far would they go to get revenge? Max knew he would ultimately have to contact his friends with the FBI, but he needed more information. He needed to know exactly who and what he was up against.

Finally, he showered and went to bed. He closed his eyes. He was not a heavy sleeper, and he had long ago adapted to only five or six hours of rest. He could exist on less if necessary, and there had been times in his life he had found it necessary.

This might be one of those times.

IT WAS AFTER 3:00 A.M. WHEN BUFORD DELIVered Jamie to the front door of a motel called the Hickory Inn, less than a mile from Jessup. Jamie's back and legs ached, and it was all she could do to reach for her purse. She had crouched on the floorboard for hours before Gunsmoke, as Jamie referred to the gun-toting man in the trailer, had cut the lights and gone to bed.

"I'll have to file a police report," Buford said, "but I'll keep your name out of it." He was apologetic.

Jamie tossed him a weary look. "Well, thanks for an evening I'm not likely to forget. I just hope I never miss a car payment." She climbed from the truck and went inside the motel. The furniture in the small lobby was old, but the place looked and smelled clean. She rang the bell three times before a woman ambled to the counter, the hair on one side of her head mashed flat, her print dress badly wrinkled. The sign on the counter read: *Mavis.*

"I'd like a room, please," Jamie said.

The woman crossed her arms, glanced at her wristwatch, and shot Jamie a dark look. "Do you happen to know what time it is?"

Jamie was in no mood to argue. "Late?"

"I closed at midnight."

"You forgot to turn your vacancy sign off."

"That's beside the point. No decent woman would check into a room at this hour unless she had monkey business on her mind."

Jamie leaned across the counter. "Mavis, I have *not* had a good night. I want a room. And don't give me a room on the second floor, because my legs are sore and I am *not* going to climb those concrete stairs. And inside that room, I want HBO like your sign says, and I want one of those cute little coffeepots, and a soft bed with clean sheets. Now, either you give me a room or I'm going to go out into that parking lot and pitch such a fit that I'll wake up every one of your guests. *That's* how bad my night has been."

Mavis grunted and slapped a registration form on the counter.

MAX ROSE AT 5:00 A.M. AND, ONCE AGAIN, checked the security monitor, computer console, and other gadgets at one end of the kitchen table where he would spend much of his time working. Outside cameras were connected to the CPU, and the monitors displayed the road leading to the cabin, as well as the surrounding property. He drank two cups of coffee, read his E-mail, and waited until the sun came up before stepping out of the front door. Electronic eyes and sophisticated motion detectors with image recognition enhancement were attached to trees and fence posts and would catch movement and set off an alarm inside the house. One of Max's employees had come in the day before to set it up, per Max's specifications.

All seemed well as Max started for the garage where he'd locked his car. He punched a series of numbers on a concealed security panel and opened the door. Muffin was waiting for him.

"How'd you sleep?" she asked. "I'll bet you didn't get a minute's rest worrying about Jamie and feeling like the biggest jerk in the world."

Max sighed. "Good morning to you, Muffin."

"See, you even sound tired. Guilt will do that to you. The first thing that goes is your appetite. Then you'll start tossing and turning all night in your bed, unable to forgive yourself for hurting someone's feelings."

"Is this going to take long?"

"Of course you're in denial right now, so you're probably OK. Once you accept the reality of the situation, all hell will break loose. Sleep deprivation, confusion, and disorientation will occur," she added. "You'll stop taking care of yourself, and your health will go to hell. Next thing you know, you've landed in the hospital with a life-threatening illness."

"I take it you're still sore with me?"

"No more than usual."

"Can we get down to business?"

"Fine. I worked all night, but I managed to get the rest of the information you asked for on Harlan Rawlins. Don't ask me how I got it or we'll both go to prison. Have you set up the printer yet?"

"Yeah, everything is up and running."

"OK, it's printing now. As for your schedule, a woman by the name of Karen Callaway will be here shortly to give you your new look, and your retired FBI pal will arrive at nine o'clock to take your picture and get your new identification in order."

"How long will it take?"

"Max, the guy is bringing his equipment in the trunk of his car. Is that quick enough for you?"

"Good old Paul. What else have you got for me?"

"You and Dave Anderson are now working part-time for Bennett Electric. Dave is bringing by a couple of uniforms later. Tom Bennett, the owner, is cooperating fully."

Max was not surprised. He had bailed Bennett Electric Company from near bankruptcy several days ago. It was sheer genius that Max's mergers and acquisitions man had managed to find it so quickly; not only had the partnership been sealed within a matter of hours, but also Max and Muffin had mapped out a business plan for Tom Bennett that promised substantial profits within a year. Tom Bennett was one grateful man, and Dave Anderson, long-time employee of Holt Industries, was a top-notch mechanical and electrical engineer who could fill in literally wherever Max needed him. Dave had already memorized the layout of Rawlins's house and was ready to move on the project.

"What about transportation?" Max asked.

"You and Dave will be sharing one of Bennett's trucks." Muffin didn't sound happy about it.

"I'm sorry I'm going to have to leave you in the garage for a few days, Muf, but my car won't exactly blend with the community."

"That's not the problem."

"I'm listening."

"Why did you call Dave Anderson in on this job? You know how he gets. He can be so obsessive-compulsive at times, he makes me crazy."

"Dave is having problems. He and his wife Melinda are divorcing."

"And we need to get involved in that for what reason?"

"Because Dave is my friend, and because he's an electrical genius who could rewire the entire White House in twenty-four hours if he had to. Besides, everybody has one or two quirks."

"OK, whatever. As far as sitting in a cool garage, that sounds good to me."

"Still having hot flashes?"

"If I get any hotter my hard drive is going into meltdown and the car's radiator will spew like a volcano."

Max nodded as though the whole thing made perfect sense. "Speaking of transportation, have you had a chance to check out a red Mustang?"

"I found a guy in New Hampshire who deals strictly with Mustangs. He has a 1964½ red convertible, black interior and top. It's a V-8 with a stick shift. The guy said it looks like it just rolled off the showroom floor, and he should know, because he's one of the top dealers in the country. I checked him out."

"I'd like to see a picture of it."

"You will. I forwarded the scanned photos to you with the rest of the stuff I'm sending to your printer. Am I good, Max, or what?"

"Damn good."

"Oh, and this guy even agreed to deliver the car personally for the right price."

"Then I suggest we pay what he's asking."

"I know what you're thinking, Max. You're thinking Jamie is going to take one look at that Mustang and forgive you. You're thinking she's going to be waiting for you with open arms when you finish up here. You're thinking see-through nighties, edible panties, and hot steamy sex, but I'm here to tell you, it isn't going to happen.

"I'm not saying don't buy the car for her;

it's your fault hers was sprayed with bullets to begin with. I know Jamie's got a thing for vintage Mustangs and that she needs transportation, but she's a proud woman and she might take it the wrong way."

"The two of you can think what you want, but my intentions are honorable. Have the guy deliver the car to the newspaper office and tell him to give the keys to Jamie's assistant, Vera Bankhead."

"You just better hope Miss Bankhead doesn't get the wrong impression. Jamie's like a daughter to her. And don't forget, that woman carries a gun."

TWO

JAMIE AWOKE TO SOMEONE POUNDING ON HER door. She was stark naked, having washed her underwear in the bathroom sink before she'd climbed into bed and fallen into an exhausted sleep. It had not occurred to her to grab her suitcase from Max's car before she'd slammed out.

Just one more thing, she thought.

Coming off the bed, she dragged the sheet with her. Her eyes were gritty, her blond hair standing out to there, and she just remembered she didn't have a toothbrush. "Who is it?" She thought her voice sounded like a frog giving birth.

"Mavis. Checkout was fifteen minutes ago. I have to clean your room."

"It's not even noon!" Jamie said.

"Not my problem."

Jamie leaned her head against the door. This was not a good sign. Here she was, tired, no clothes or car, and she was about to get thrown out of a second-rate motel. It was starting out to be a really sucky morning. Finally, she raised her head, and, keeping the chain in place, she cracked the door. The sun hit her between the eyes. "I'm requesting a late checkout," Jamie said.

"I'll have to charge you for another night."

Jamie just looked at Mavis. She wore pink sponge curlers beneath a gauzy scarf, and her rouge stood out on her pasty skin, two perfectly round circles that looked as though they'd been pressed on with an ink stamp. She was enjoying herself, Jamie decided.

Mavis tapped one foot impatiently.

"It'll take me a minute to get dressed," Jamie told her. She closed the door and hurried to the coffeepot. She dropped the filter into the top, added water, and stepped inside the bathroom. Her panties were still damp. "Oh, great," she muttered, thinking it was just another sign that her morning wasn't going to be all that great.

She slipped them on anyway, threw on her jeans and top, and filled a thick paper cup with coffee. She was still sipping it when she stepped out her door a few minutes later. She found Mavis waiting with a maid's cart.

"Is there a taxi service in this town?" Jamie asked.

Mavis looked her up and down. "Are those the same clothes you had on last night?"

"Yes, but I washed my underwear," Jamie blurted before she had time to think. She sighed. "Yes, they are. Why?"

"Are you in trouble with the law?"

"Not yet."

Mavis gave her a long look. "Dixie Cab Service. Phone calls are a dollar."

Jamie fished a dollar bill from her purse, hurried back into the room, and grabbed the telephone book. She dialed the number for a taxi just as Mavis turned on the vacuum cleaner.

"THIS IS IT," THE CABDRIVER ANNOUNCED A half hour later as he pulled into the parking lot of Bud's Used Cars. Jamie paid him and climbed from the battered cab.

She made her way toward a small construction trailer where a sign read: *Bad Credit? No Problem.* She opened the trailer door and was hit with a blast of cold air blowing from a sputtering window unit. Jamie found a man sitting at his desk, holding a cigar in one hand and sipping coffee from a chipped mug with the words *Do Me* in his other.

He stood so fast he almost spilled his coffee. "Good morning, miss," he said. "I'm Bud Herzog. What can I do for you this fine day?"

"I need a car. Something cheap but reliable."

"Well then, you've come to the right place. Matter of fact, I got several good, clean cars coming in day after tomorrow."

"I need something today. Now."

"Oh, well." Bud chewed his cigar. "I'm a little low on inventory, but you're welcome to look. You interested in a Cadillac? It's twelve years old, but it's solid. Low mileage."

Jamie thought about it. "I'm not really the Cadillac type."

"You're absolutely right. You need something sporty. Come with me, I've got just the car." He led her outside to a shiny red vehicle. "Now, this here is a Camaro RS. Fully loaded, got all the extras. It's a 1997 model, has a few miles on it, but it runs like a charm. Used to be owned by an old schoolteacher."

Jamie shot him a sideways glance. "An old schoolteacher, huh?"

"Yep. Liberian, I believe she was," he added, mispronouncing the word. "She took real good care of it."

Jamie peered inside the window. "It's got one hundred and sixty thousand miles on it!"

"Yeah, she had to commute to work."

"How much?"

"This one goes for twenty-one hundred dollars, but I'm going to give you my rock-bottom price and sell it to you for fifteen. Is that a deal or what?"

Jamie gaped at him. "I can't afford to spend that kind of money. Don't you have something under five hundred dollars?"

Bud looked surprised. "Hon, you can't buy a good bicycle for under five hundred bucks. Not these days, anyhow." He suddenly looked hurt. "I'm cutting my profit to the bone here, darlin'."

Jamie checked out several other cars, but they were even more expensive. She spied an old pickup truck parked on the last row. "How much for that truck?"

Bud looked surprised. "I plumb forgot about that old thing. My cousin brought it in last night, and I haven't had a chance to clean it up. I don't think you'd be happy with it."

"How come?"

"It's old and beat-up. You can see it's got a lot of rust on it. There's a hole in the floorboard on the passenger's side, but my cousin nailed plywood to it so his kids wouldn't fall out. Mostly, he used it to carry hunting dogs. He's a big coon hunter."

Jamie walked toward the truck. "Just how old is it?"

"Early eighties. It's a Dodge, and they hold up pretty good, but I wouldn't feel right selling it to you."

Jamie opened the door and winced at the sight. On the driver's side, the leather seat was split and the stuffing had spilled out. Papers and fast-food bags littered the floor. "Mileage is high," she noted. "Does it run?"

Bud nodded. "Pretty good."

"How does it look under the hood?"

"Well, my cousin is a mechanic, so he's careful to change the oil and transmission fluid and keep everything in working order. He rebuilt the engine some five or six years ago, but it's still an old truck."

"Do you think it'll get me to Knoxville?"

"You know any shortcuts?" He laughed. When Jamie didn't join in, his look sobered. "Yeah, I reckon it'll get you where you're going."

"How much?"

Bud shrugged. "As is? I reckon I could let you have it for six hundred dollars."

Jamie blinked. "Excuse me, but are we talking about the same truck?"

"OK, OK, I'll sell it to you for four hundred dollars, but I can't give you a warranty at that price."

Jamie glanced at the bed in back. And found herself looking into the face of one of the ugliest bloodhounds she'd ever seen. He had a wrinkled forlorn face, mournful eyes, and long ears. Skin hung in loose, pendulous folds, as though he had never quite managed to fill his own hide.

"What's with the dog?" she asked.

"Oh, yeah, I forgot. He comes with the truck."

She blinked at Bud. "What do you mean, he comes with the truck?"

"He's kinda attached to it. My cousin asked me to take him to the animal shelter, but I didn't have the heart. He wouldn't last long there. He has, uh, problems."

Jamie looked more closely at the animal. "What kinds of problems?"

Bud toyed with his cigar, rolling it between his thumb and forefinger. "Well, he's deaf in one ear, and his eyesight ain't what it used to be. He's also suffering shell shock."

"Shell shock?"

"Like I said, my cousin did a lot of coon hunting. This here dog wasn't much of a hunter; in fact, he runs at the sight of a raccoon and hunkers down in the nearest ditch if someone fires a gun."

"He's losing his hair."

Bud shrugged. "Way I heared it, he was attacked by a big old grandpappy coon. Hair never grew back. My cousin says he whimpers in his sleep. Says he thinks the dog has flashbacks. You ask me, I think he's suffering from that-there post-traumatic stress disorder."

Jamie rolled her eyes heavenward. "Oh, brother!"

"And he hates country-western music. I need to tell you that up front. He goes bananas when he hears it."

"I'll agree to buy the truck, but I'm not taking the dog."

The hound suddenly let out a pitiful howl as though he'd understood what Jamie had said.

"It's nothing personal," Jamie said before realizing she was talking to a dog. She shook her head sadly.

The animal covered his face with his paws.

"Uh-oh," Bud said. "I think you hurt his feelings."

"Oh, jeez." Jamie pulled Bud aside. "Look, I've never owned an animal, not even a gold-fish. I can't keep a houseplant alive."

"Oh, Fleas ain't no trouble, honey. You just give him a little food and water and he's fine. Mostly all he does is sleep."

"His name is Fleas?"

"Yeah, that's what my cousin calls him. But I personally checked him out. There ain't nary a flea on this hound's body, I can promise you that."

Jamie looked thoughtful. Damn. Just what she *didn't* need, a dog with physical and emo-tional problems, not to mention one who freaked out at the sound of gunfire, which she seemed to draw like fruit did flies. "I can't do this," she said.

"OK, tell you what. You take the truck *and* the dog, and I'll knock off fifty bucks."

JAMIE ARRIVED IN SWEET PEA, TENNESSEE, shortly after 5:00 P.M., just as a light mist be-gan to fall. Oh, great, she thought. And her with a dog in the back of her truck. She stopped at a red light and glanced over her shoulder. Fleas had his nose pressed against the back window, fogging it with his breath.

"It's OK, boy," she said loudly, even though she suspected he couldn't hear her.

She had to admit he'd been a good traveler. She'd stopped twice to give him water and let him go to the bathroom, and she'd ordered him a cheeseburger at a fast-food restaurant when she'd stopped for lunch. Probably wasn't a proper diet for a dog; she needed to buy the poor animal real dog food. It was up to her to see that he ate right until she could find him a good home. Not that it would be easy finding somebody interested in adopting a dog with emotional problems and missing hair.

Jamie could just imagine what Vera would say about her becoming a dog owner. Sixty-year-old Vera Bankhead, her secretary, whom Jamie had recently promoted to assistant editor out of fear and intimidation, was the closest thing Jamie'd had to a mother and was not above telling her how to run her life. "Jamie," she'd say. "You have absolutely no business taking on a dog. Why, you can't even take care of yourself."

This was due to the fact Jamie's cupboards and refrigerator were always bare. She seldom took time to buy groceries, except for coffee and junk food. And when she'd picked up her father's smoking habit, Vera had hit the ceiling. She had promptly declared the *Beaumont Gazette* a smoke-free environment, so that if Jamie wanted an occasional cigarette she had to smoke it outside come rain or cold weather. Jamie had kicked the habit, only to pick it up again briefly during the past two weeks, when her stress level had been at an all-time high. Dodging bullets could put a big strain on the nervous system, she reminded herself.

Vera would be proud to know Jamie was now making a concerted effort to keep her body as smoke-free as the newspaper office, although she had certainly craved a cigarette when she and Buford Noll had waited out the rifle-bearing lunatic in the mobile home.

Jamie thought of Vera. The woman would not appreciate Jamie just taking off without telling a soul. Which was why Jamie had called her from Max's cell phone when she knew the woman would be out. "I'm taking a well-deserved vacation," she'd said.

Vera would never fall for it, of course. She'd never fallen for what she'd termed Jamie's "shenanigans" during Jamie's youth and wouldn't fall for this latest scheme. It didn't matter that Jamie had already celebrated her thirtieth birthday; there would be hell to pay when she returned to Beaumont.

The mist turned to rain. Jamie needed to find a place to stop for the night. She drove a long stretch of highway before she spied a tired-looking motel in faded aqua cinderblock with black wrought-iron railing. She passed it, then, after driving a few more miles in the downpour without spotting other lodging, turned back. She suspected there weren't many motels in a town the size of Sweet Pea.

Jamie turned into the parking lot a few minutes later and pulled beneath a covered area in front. She climbed from the truck and managed to convince Fleas to get inside the cab of the pickup. The dog was shivering despite the summer temperatures. She had a feeling he was merely playing on her sympathy, even though he didn't look that smart. She dried him as best she could with an old towel she found stuffed behind the seat. He looked downright pitiful, what with his big soulful eyes and drooping skin. She was already proving to be a lousy pet owner.

"Bless your heart, you've got a face only a mother could love," she told him, rolling her window all the way down so he would get plenty of air while she was gone. "Now, stay down. If the motel manager sees you we'll never get a room."

The littered grassy area in front of the motel, as well as the badly smudged double-glass doors leading inside, should have prepared Jamie for the lobby area. The smell of cooked onions greeted her, someone obviously preparing dinner in a back room. The carpet needed to be vacuumed, and the man behind the counter wore a stained shirt. He didn't seem to hear Jamie enter; his eyes were fixed on a TV set attached high on a wall.

Jamie stepped up to the counter. "Excuse me, but is this the only motel in town?"

The man looked at her. "Why would you ask me a question like that? Is this place not good enough for you?"

"No, it's fine. I just—" Jamie was suddenly interrupted by the sound of a barking dog. It was not just any dog. Fleas had decided to follow her. Damn.

"Is that your dog?" the man asked.

"What dog?"

"The one scratching on the glass door."

Jamie glanced over her shoulder. "I've never seen that dog before in my life. Do you have HBO or Showtime?"

"No, and I'm going to have to charge you

ten bucks extra for that mutt on account I'll have to spray the room after you leave."

"Yeah, OK." Jamie reached inside her purse for her credit card. It might not be the best motel, it might not have HBO or Showtime, but it was probably the only place in town that would take a homely-looking bloodhound.

Jamie checked in, grabbed her key, and joined Fleas outside. He wagged his tail as though happy to see her. "Thanks a lot," she muttered. "You just cost me ten bucks." She spied the newspaper stand and purchased a paper, then stopped by a couple of vending machines for cheese crackers and a soft drink. "At least I won't have to cook dinner tonight," she told the dog, who seemed to take a sudden interest in the crackers.

She followed the numbers on the doors, counting the way toward her room. A big man stepped out from behind one of the doors and looked her up and down. He wore a grimy T-shirt and bore tattoos on both arms. Jamie offered him a stiff smile as she stepped up to the door next to his. Just her luck; they were neighbors. Not that she was surprised. It wasn't likely she was going to run into any doctors or lawyers in a dump like this.

He made kissing sounds.

Jamie rolled her eyes and looked at him. "Please don't do that," she said, slipping the key into the lock.

He grinned. "You staying here?"

Jamie's look was deadpan as she tried to turn the key. It wouldn't budge. "No, actually I'm trying to break into this room so I can get decorating ideas."

He stepped closer. "Is that your dog?"

"Yeah, and he'll tear your leg off if you come near me."

"Might be worth it. How about a drink later? I got a bottle of Wild Turkey in my room."

"It certainly sounds tempting, but my boy-friend, Killer, is picking me up for an AA meeting in ten minutes. Sorry." The key finally turned and Jamie opened the door. "Have a nice evening." She went inside and waited for Fleas to follow before locking the door and putting the chain in place. She shoved a chair in front of the door to be safe.

"This is just wonderful," Jamie said, glaring at Fleas. "Because of you I am reduced to stay-ing in a hovel with dangerous-looking people. I'll never get any sleep tonight."

His tail thumped against the ugly carpet.

Jamie glanced about. The room was clean enough but drab and depressing with its faded moss green walls and brown bedspread. Even Fleas seemed to give it a second glance. He sank onto the floor and stared at her crackers.

Jamie sat on the bed, opened the crackers, and shared them with him. He swallowed each one without chewing. "If we live through the night, we're checking out first thing in the morning." She opened the newspaper, skimmed the articles. One article particularly caught her eye.

"Holy hell!" she blurted. "Reverend Harlan Rawlins is preaching at seven o'clock tonight at Sweet Pea Community Church." She looked up in alarm. "I don't have anything to wear. I don't even have extra underwear. And that's not the worst of it. The worst of it is I'm talking to a dog. How sick is that?"

Jamie jumped up from the bed and peered out the curtain. The rain had abated and her neighbor, Brutus, was nowhere in sight. She looked at Fleas, debating whether or not to take him with her. If she left him behind he'd probably start barking, and they'd get kicked out. "Come on. We're going shopping." She grabbed her purse, opened the door, and they made a run for it.

SWEET PEA COMMUNITY CHURCH WAS FILLED to capacity when Max arrived with Dave Anderson, both dressed in uniform.

Dave was a slender man with light brown hair and tortoiseshell glasses that had a tendency to slide down his nose. He and Max stood along the back wall of the church, scanning the crowd. A massive navy banner hung on the wall above the choir, the words *Love Ministry* emblazoned in white letters.

"Do you have any idea how many germs are in this place?" Dave whispered, shoving his glasses upward with his pointer finger.

Max shrugged. "Rawlins is offering miracle healing toward the end of the service. You might want to get in line."

"Very funny," Dave replied.

Max caught sight of a tall redhead in sunglasses who seemed to be making a fuss in her attempt to get a front row seat. He leaned sideways to get a better look.

She wore a short denim skirt and a tight fire engine red tank top that fit snug against lush breasts and left very little to a man's imagination. Her stilettos showed off a pair of long, shapely legs that had captured the attention of most of, if not the entire, congregation. Rhine-stones dangled from her ears and flashed each time she moved her head. She turned slightly, snatched off her sunglasses, and mouthed something to a heavy woman who seemed to be giving her the most trouble.

Max frowned. Even if she was in disguise, it would have been impossible for him not to recognize Jamie Swift. "I don't believe it," he muttered under his breath.

Dave leaned close. "What is it?"

"Trouble," Max said.

THE CONGREGATION BURST INTO THE HYMN "Bringing in the Sheaves" as Jamie finally managed to squeeze herself between two people. She held her head high and ignored the looks of disapproval coming from the women around her, even as their husbands tried not to stare. Not that she blamed them. Her slut suit, as she had referred to it to Fleas, was way over the line, as was her wild hair. The wig had cost more than she'd planned to spend, but it looked like the real enchilada. She had *floozy* written all over her. She only hoped Harlan Rawlins noticed.

Her plan depended on it.

REVEREND HARLAN RAWLINS APPEARED DURing the last stanza of the song. He carried a cordless microphone, and he joined the singing. He had a strong, well-modulated voice, and he sang with confidence. Jamie studied him closely. She wasn't sure what she'd expected, but she certainly hadn't expected him to be so handsome and polished. Vera had taken Jamie to a couple of tent revivals when she was young, but those ministers wore cheap suits and yelled a lot.

Harlan Rawlins did not look like any minister she had ever seen. He looked like a movie star. But there was more to him than good looks. The man had presence. He exuded such charisma that it was easy to see why people followed him, why women might find it difficult to say no to his advances. The air seemed electrified, and Jamie could literally feel his energy from where she sat. She needed to remember the exact feelings he evoked so she could make note of them later. Her readers would want to know what it was about the man that had made him so successful, that made people dig deep inside their pockets to support his ministry.

Jamie was so focused on the man that she was only vaguely aware of the shuffling of feet behind her.

Someone tapped her on the shoulder. Jamie glanced over her shoulder and gaped at the sight of Max Holt.

THREE

Max looked different, his hair in a buzz cut, face unshaven. She dropped her gaze to his uniform where the name Bennett Electric was stitched across his shirt pocket. Jamie wasn't surprised to find him in disguise; what shocked her was the fact he could pull it all off and still look sexy as all get-out. She realized Max was staring at her as well.

"What are you doing here?" he demanded in a whisper.

"I'm here for the same reason you are," she replied.

Several people turned and glared at them. "Shhh!" the lady beside her said.

Jamie suddenly remembered how things had ended between Max and her the night before.

"Go away," she whispered. She turned and faced the front, but the hair on her neck prickled. She could feel Max's eyes on her. Well, let him take a good look at the new Jamie Swift, she thought.

The song ended, but Harlan remained quiet and smiling. His eyes scanned the congregation; he nodded at several people he seemed to recognize.

"Brothers and sisters, it is great to be back in Sweet Pea, Tennessee," he said. The crowd cheered. Jamie felt something at her ear.

"Why are you dressed like a hooker?" Max asked.

The people were so busy clapping that those around her didn't seem to notice. "I'm here to get my story, Max," she replied.

"Dressed like that?"

She smiled and fluttered her long lashes. They were as fake as the cleavage that peeked over her tank top. Funny what a pair of false eyelashes and a good push-up bra could do. "Yes."

The woman beside Jamie nudged her. Jamie tossed her a dirty look but faced the front once more.

Harlan waited until the people sat and grew quiet before speaking again. "I have been on the road for weeks, living out of motel rooms and counting off the days until my return. I'm home with my family and friends now, sleeping in my own bed, and eating home-cooked meals. Praise God!"

This time the congregation laughed and applauded, and Harlan laughed with them, his smile enhanced by beautiful teeth that shone a bright white against his tanned face. Jamie thought he looked like he belonged in a toothpaste commercial. His navy suit, obviously tailor-made, emphasized a fit body and brought out his blond hair.

"Dorothy was right," he said. "There's no place like home." More applause. After a moment, he grew serious and closed his eyes. "Let us pray."

When the prayer ended, Rawlins walked out to the very edge of the platform. He had a habit of pausing before he spoke, as though waiting for every eye to see him, every ear to hear what he had to say.

"You know, brothers and sisters, this ministry has surely been blessed. We've fed thousands through our outreach program, and each year our young people travel to the poorest areas, patching holes in rooftops, installing windows where families have nothing more to keep the cold out than plastic or cardboard. Yet there are still folks, our neighbors, mind you, who don't have inside plumbing or electricity. But God bless our local volunteers who have gone into these homes and donated their skills so these poor people can enjoy many of the things some of us take for granted." Another pause. "But you know, feeding people and keeping them dry and warm isn't enough.

"Someone once asked Mother Teresa what people needed most in this world, and she had a surprising answer." He looked about the congregation. "What do *you* think is the single greatest need people have today, brothers and sisters?" Harlan folded his hands behind his back and paced the stage. "You know if someone had asked me that question, I would have had to think about it.

"We see pictures of starving people in third world countries, children in cancer wards and burn centers who live with pain on a daily basis, and we see single parents trying to play both mama and daddy because of the staggering divorce rates. Many of these parents can't afford child care, so the children are left to fend for themselves. And when boys and girls don't have adequate supervision, they get into bad trouble. Where do you think they end up?"

"In jail!" a man shouted from the audience.

"Yes, sir," Harlan replied. "These kids get addicted to drugs, and they commit all sorts of crimes in order to support their habits." Harlan looked sad. "These young people are filling our prisons today."

He walked over to the podium, pulled a handkerchief from his pocket, and mopped his eyes. "Please forgive me," he said. "This is not the sermon I had planned to give. I didn't prepare for it. But I spent a long time in prayer this morning, and this is the sermon the Lord gave me."

Harlan gazed across the crowd, and when he spoke, his voice was soft, barely a whisper. "But Mother Teresa was not as concerned about hunger or illness or the breakup of families. The woman who witnessed the absolute worst in human misery, who lived among the poorest of the poor, and who saw every horrific disease known to man was more concerned with a different affliction, and that affliction, brothers and sisters, was loneliness."

Harlan raised his voice on the next sentence, and he began to speak quickly, as though he couldn't get the words out fast enough. "Loneliness. That feeling of isolation and the thought that nobody cares. It eats through the human heart and soul like maggots, because when people suffer loneliness they feel unloved, and when there is no love, there is *nothing*!" Harlan pounded on the podium and shouted the word. "Nothing!"

People in the congregation shouted, "Amen!"

Harlan jumped from the stage and walked down the aisle, and the crowd turned in their seats in order to see him. He stood by the back door. "I'll say it again!" he shouted. "Where there is no love, there is nothing!

"Love *does* conquer all, brethren. Where there is love, there is no loneliness. Where there is love, there is *hope*." The crowd cheered, once again rising from their seats.

Harlan hurried toward the front of the church and climbed the stairs to the stage. The congregation continued to cheer.

"*Love,* brothers and sisters. I get excited just saying the word. *L-o-v-e,*" he spelled out. "The same love that God showed us when he gave his only begotten son so that we should not perish but have life everlasting. Shout Amen!"

The crowd began shouting the word. The choir broke into a rousing gospel song. Music blasted through the church, and Harlan began to dance as he gazed toward the heavens, arms lifted high in the air. He clapped his hands, keeping time to the music, and the choir members joined him, dancing and reaching their arms toward the heavens. The congregation began to dance as well.

As the last chords faded, Harlan became serious. "I'm going to make an unusual request tonight," he said. "I know this ministry needs funds to keep it running, and I know there are starving people in distant lands, but tonight I'm asking you to make a love offering for those in your town who don't know where their next meal is coming from. For your neighbors," he added. "For those sad faces we see standing in front of the unemployment office, for the boys and girls who attend schools with holes in their shoes. Many of those who are standing in this congregation tonight," he added softly.

"I am not going to collect one dime for this ministry while I'm in town, and I'm not going to send the money away to some country you've never even heard of. The money you give tonight will stay right here in Sweet Pea, and I aim to see that it fills those bare cupboards and that our children have what they need. That's what we're all about, dear folks. Love Ministry is all about loving and giving, and that is what chases away loneliness.

"Now I know there are some who can't afford to give much, and to you I'd say this: The Lord knows your heart. Follow your heart. And for every penny you give, this ministry will match it tenfold."

The people applauded.

Jamie looked around, noted the hopeful expressions on the faces of those around her. They believed in Harlan Rawlins. He had reeled them in. Damn, he was so good.

Jamie turned and looked at Max. He met her gaze, and she could see her own thoughts mirrored in his eyes. He did not like Harlan Rawlins. Max, like Jamie, was wondering how a man could prey on people who had nothing else to give.

"It's not enough to chop wood for a fire to keep a family warm," Harlan said. "You need to go out there and set their hearts on fire for Jesus!"

More music, more dancing.

"Does anyone here need a miracle tonight?" Harlan shouted above the din, drawing Jamie's attention to the front once more.

The crowd cried out.

Harlan smiled. "Some of you, perhaps many of you, know that I was converted at an early age. I was only ten years old when God sent me a vision that I was to preach to the world, that I was to go forth and heal in his name. Let God grant you a miracle tonight, brothers and sisters. Allow God, who has chosen me, a simple preacher, a sinner of the worst kind, to act as his vessel. Come to Jesus!"

People began lining up in the aisle. Jamie hesitated only a moment before she joined them. She could feel Max's eyes boring into her. He was, no doubt, wondering what she was up to. So let him wonder.

Harlan spoke to a man at the front of the line and then raised his microphone to his lips. "Brothers and sisters, we have a man who suffers chronic back pain and is unable to work. He has sought the help of doctors to no avail. Well, I will tell you, there is a power that can heal all pain and suffering. This power doesn't have medical degrees on his walls and he doesn't have to put us through rigorous tests to find out what's wrong, because he knows what ails us before we ask. Bow your heads, brethren, and let's pray for a miracle."

The people bowed their heads, and Harlan put his hands on the man's back and said a prayer for him. Jamie watched closely. For all she knew, the man could have been planted in the crowd to make it look as though Harlan was actually capable of healing the sick. For all she knew, there could be dozens planted in the congregation for the same reason.

After much praying, Harlan raised his hands and shouted, "Receive your miracle, brother!" Harlan ordered the man to touch his toes, and the man touched his toes, not once but several times. The crowd became jubilant as Harlan moved on to the next person.

After fifteen minutes of waiting in line, Jamie stepped up to Harlan. She was nervous, her palms damp. She wiped them on her denim skirt. "I am a sinner, Reverend," she said quietly.

"You're in the right place, sister. We welcome sinners here." Harlan perused her from head to toe, and his bright blue eyes flickered with interest. "Are you looking for a miracle tonight?"

She nodded. "I need to be healed of an addiction."

"What's your name, dear lady?"

"Jane." Jamie winced inwardly; it was the first name that came to mind. Probably would have served her better if she'd used a sexier name.

Harlan put one hand on her shoulder and held up the other. "Brothers and sisters, we have a woman here who wants to be cured from an addiction. Now, I don't know if she is addicted to drugs or alcohol or both, but God doesn't care, because he can whip the worst of them. You don't have to go to the Betty Ford Center to get well. God only asks that you kneel before him. 'Ask and ye shall receive,' the Bible tells us."

Harlan returned his gaze to Jamie. "Sister, what addiction would you like for the Lord to take from you tonight?" he asked.

Jamie covered the microphone with one hand. "It's, um, really, really personal."

Harlan didn't bat an eye. "The Lord forgives even the worst of us."

She hung her head. She could smell Harlan's cologne, feel the heat from his body. "I'm a, well, a woman who can't seem to get enough of . . ." She didn't finish.

Harlan was obviously hanging on to her every word. "Say it, sister."

"It's an *s* word. I'm too embarrassed to tell you." It had seemed so easy when Jamie had rehearsed it in front of the mirror in the motel room and again in her rearview mirror as she'd applied her new lipstick called Oral Promise. *I'm a sex addict. I'm a sex addict.* But now the words wouldn't come.

And dressed as she was, with her breasts shoved up to her chin, she figured Harlan Rawlins had to be about as dumb as they came not to figure it out.

"Turn around and face your brothers and sisters and tell them, dear woman. The Lord says you must confess your sins in order to be forgiven. Tell us what this *s* word is that fills you with such shame you can't even utter it."

Jamie faced the expectant crowd. All eyes were focused on her. "I, uh, um . . ."

"Say it, sister!" a woman yelled.

Jamie's heart pounded in her chest. "I like to, um . . ." She paused and took a deep breath. "Shop!" she finally cried.

The people looked about as though confused.

Jamie did a mental head slap. She had blown it. People would see her as a fake; she would never get close to Harlan. She didn't dare look in Max's direction.

The crowd was quiet, the look on Harlan's face confused. Jamie's face burned with embarrassment. "I'm a shopaholic!" she shouted. "I know it doesn't sound so bad, but I can't control my spending. I see a half-price sale and I get all tingly. I'll buy everything on the table whether I need it or not. If I see a sweater on sale, I can't just buy one, I buy ten. My husband cut up all my credit cards, but I went out and got new ones. The bank foreclosed on our house. We can't afford food."

She finally had their attention. Jamie grabbed Harlan's microphone. "I am addicted to blue light specials and red dot sales. I can't resist a bargain."

"We understand, sister," Harlan said, reaching for his microphone.

Jamie held it aside. She was on a roll. "I'm so . . ." She paused and hung her head. "Sick!"

The crowd nodded sympathetically.

From his place in the second row, Max rolled his eyes and shook his head sadly. In the back, Dave edged away from a man who was scratching himself.

Jamie turned and raised her eyes to Rawlins's. Still holding the microphone, she covered it with one hand so that the congregation could not hear her words. "What I just said was a lie," she whispered. "I'm not really a shopaholic. I'm a sex addict. I just couldn't bear to tell everyone."

Two blond brows shot high on his head. Sweat beaded his brow. "I'm sorry for putting you on the spot."

Jamie swallowed. "I'm so ashamed."

He put his hand on her shoulder, and he squeezed it, massaged it, actually. "Brothers and sisters, we have heard this young lady's confession, and we both know how hard it is to battle an addiction." He turned to Jamie, and his eyes were bright with interest. "Sister, are you willing to go into private counseling with me in order to beat this?" he asked. "Because you know with the Lord's help we can lick it once and for all."

"I'll do anything," she said. She fluttered her lashes, hoping they didn't stick to her cheek. "Anything."

Harlan swallowed so hard his Adam's apple bobbed erratically. "I'll speak with you after the service."

Jamie saw the promise in his gaze that made her suspect he wasn't exactly thinking along spiritual lines. "Oh, thank you." She clasped his hand tightly, bent down, and kissed it. The crowd applauded. She lingered for a moment, letting her warm breath fan over Harlan's skin, and she was almost certain he shivered.

Jamie reclaimed her seat in the front row. It was all she could do to keep from grinning. "Gotcha," she whispered.

JAMIE EXITED THE CHURCH SOME MINUTES later after setting an appointment with Rawlins for the next day. She headed straight for her truck, where Fleas waited. Danged if she wasn't beginning to like the dog. That didn't mean she planned to keep him. He needed to live on a farm where he'd have plenty of space to run. Not that she'd actually seen him run or even move at a fast pace, mind you. He sort of ambled about. Mostly he slept.

Jamie suddenly felt a presence. Max.

He grabbed her wrist. "Oh, no, you don't."

Jamie turned. Had they not been surrounded by people, God-fearing church folks, she would have let him have it right there. After what she'd been through she was ready for a showdown. Instead, she very politely extricated herself from his grasp.

"Max, I'm only going to say this once. Get out of my face *and* my life."

"What do you think you're doing here?" he demanded.

"Going after a story, that's what."

"I specifically told you—"

Jamie hated that she still found him so attractive. "I don't give a rat's tail what you told me, Holt," she said. "Go away."

"Not until you explain that outfit. But first, let's start with the hair."

Jamie hitched her chin high.

"Not that it's any of your business, but this outfit, not to mention the wig, is designed specifically to entice Harlan Rawlins. It's all part of my plan to get close to him. Learn his secrets."

"How did you get here?"

Jamie was thankful he hadn't pushed for more information with regard to her plan. "I bought a truck." She motioned to the pickup. Fleas's head was propped on the side, and he was drooling.

"Damn, Jamie, that's the ugliest thing I've ever laid eyes on."

He could be so annoying, she thought. Max Holt had a way of getting under her skin in the worst way. "So it has a little rust on it. I got it for a steal."

"I'm talking about the dog."

"Don't bad-mouth my dog, Holt," she said. "It just so happens he's pure bloodhound. Comes from a family of champions."

"Right."

"And I figured I needed a guard dog."

Max looked dumbfounded as he glanced from the dog back to her. "A guard dog? Looks like he couldn't catch a dried biscuit. You know, you're taking a huge risk being here. This could be dangerous."

Jamie crossed her arms in a businesslike manner. "I have to do it, Max. I need the story for my newspaper. And I'm following my dream."

"Your dream is to dress like a hooker and drive a junk heap?" he asked.

"Very funny. I had a lot of time to think during my drive here, and I realized I needed to make some changes in my life. I'm tired of writing about high school football games and city council meetings. I want a story with some meat in it. As for the way I'm dressed, I'm on assignment."

"You sound pretty serious about this."

"I've spent my life doing what was expected of me." Which was true, she reminded herself. She'd spent years taking care of a sick father and trying to save the family newspaper from one calamity after another. "I'm done with people-pleasing, Max. From now on, I only have to please myself."

"I'm glad to hear it, Jamie," Max said. "It's about time you started thinking about yourself. But we still need to talk." He glanced toward the truck he and Dave were sharing and found his friend leaning against it, watching the crowd. Max waved, managing to get his attention. "I'll catch up with you later!" he called out to the man. Dave nodded, climbed into the truck, and drove away.

"Here, give me the keys to your truck," Max said. "We can talk at my cabin."

"Excuse me?" Jamie snatched the keys from his reach.

"I think it's great, what you're doing, but I refuse to stand by and allow you to put yourself in danger."

Jamie waved a hand in front of him. "Hello-o-o? Did you already forget what I just told you? I'm doing this for me. Besides, you dumped me."

"I did not dump you. You jumped out of my car and refused to get back in."

Jamie noticed they were drawing stares. She hitched her chin high. "Look, Max, I don't want to make a scene, OK? But if you don't leave me alone I'm going to have to slug you."

He grinned. "You wouldn't really hit me."

She hated when he grinned like that. It just emphasized his sexiness. She could almost imagine her bones getting soft under her skin. Trouble was he knew exactly what he was doing to her. "What do you want, Max? You only grin like that when you want something."

The smile turned lazy. "What I want and what I need are two separate things, but would you at least give me a lift back to my cabin? My ride just drove away."

FOUR

"YOUR RIDE LEFT YOU?" SHE SAID. "SOUNDS like you got a problem, Bubba."

Max arched a brow. *"Bubba?"*

"All right, I'll give you a ride if you'll promise not to say anything to annoy me."

He looked thoughtful. "I'm not sure that's possible."

Jamie almost laughed. "Put some effort into it. And no more wisecracks about my dog."

They climbed into the truck, and Jamie started the engine.

"This thing is pretty rough inside," Max said.

"See that, you've already done it. Annoyed the hell out of me."

"Only because you're still angry with me because I didn't think you should get involved in this, er, job."

"In order to be angry with you, I would have to be emotionally invested, and that's just not the case."

He chuckled. "Face it, Swifty. You're still hot for me."

"I can't hear you," Jamie said, turning on the radio. All she got was static. She pushed the button, and a country-western song came on. Max started to say something, and she turned up the volume to drown him out. She was not going to let him goad her. All at once, Fleas pounced against the window and began growling.

"What the hell?" Max said.

Jamie hit the brake and turned around in her seat. Fleas's teeth were bared. He clawed the glass as though trying to get at Max. "Oh, damn, I forgot. He hates country-western music." She turned off the radio.

Max stared, open-mouthed.

She glanced over her shoulder. "Sit!" she ordered the dog.

Fleas paced for a moment, then sank onto the bed of the truck. Jamie turned and caught Max's astonished look. "He hates country-western music," she repeated.

"I'll try to keep that in mind. Turn right once you pull out of the parking lot."

Jamie did as she was told. The truck bounced along the pockmarked road.

"Where are you staying?" Max asked.

"I found a motel in town."

Max looked surprised. "In Sweet Pea? Dave said there were only two places. One is being repainted, and the other one is a dump."

Jamie offered him a grim look. "That means Dave and I are staying at the same place."

"No, he's staying in Knoxville. I offered him the spare room at my place, but the mattresses and pillows are stuffed with feathers. Dave has allergies. You're welcome to use the spare room, Jamie."

"No, thanks."

"It would be easier if we worked together. We could share information. I have a complete printout on Rawlins, the kind of information you can't get anywhere else."

Jamie looked at him. "I'm not going to ask how many laws you broke getting it. What kind of information?"

"I'll let you look through it if you like."

Oh, he was a cool one, Jamie thought. "I can find out what I need on my own."

"Whatever you say, Swifty."

"I told you to stop calling me that."

"It suits you." His voice dropped. "Especially now that you've got all that curly red hair. And I'll have to admit that skirt does your legs justice."

"Don't start, Max." Nevertheless, her stomach did a quick flip-flop at the thought.

"You're one of those women who look good in everything," he said. "I'll bet you look even better in nothing."

"I should have made you ride in the back with the dog."

Max merely smiled.

They rode in silence for a few minutes. Jamie wondered what kind of information Max had. It *would* make her job easier if she knew exactly what she was up against, but that would mean playing ball with him again, and that's the last thing she wanted to do. Max Holt played fast and loose, took way too many chances. If that weren't stressful enough, he seemed to have trouble with the word *no*.

Yes sir, she was better off on her own.

"What did you think of Rawlins's sermon tonight?" Max asked after a minute.

"He certainly has stage presence."

"He has to be good in order to steal all that

money. Those poor people are so desperate
they'll believe anything."

"People need hope. Harlan gives it to them."

"You're not falling for any of that holy ba-
loney, are you?"

"Of course not. I'm just telling you why he's
able to get away with all that he does."

"I saw the way you were staring at him.
Don't forget what he tried to do to us."

"If I was staring, it was because I was trying
to get a fix on him. I have to be objective here.
We don't know that he was responsible for ordering the hit, and we don't know that he's
scamming people. All we have are suspicions."

"Trust me, he's as greedy as the people he
does business with."

"Nevertheless, he is helping the community.
Oh, I'm sure he's skimming money, but some
of it is actually going to a fine cause. Did you
take a good look at the people in that church,
Max? They live in poverty." She looked at
him. "I don't expect you to understand what
being poor is like." Not that she'd actually
been poor, but she had certainly lived on the
fringes from time to time.

"I've seen poverty, Jamie. I've seen much
worse than this. And I've tried to help people."

Jamie stared straight ahead. She knew he

spoke the truth. Max Holt might be an ego-maniac and the world's worst womanizer, but one only had to pick up a newspaper to see that he did more than his share of giving. He pumped millions into various research facilities and children's hospitals, and he'd started a watchdog program that badgered companies that refused to spend the kind of money nec-essary to control pollution.

"I know you do your share, Max. I don't mean to sound like I'm picking on you; I just despise seeing people taken advantage of. Es-pecially when they have nothing to begin with," she added. "I don't know how Rawlins lives with himself, and I don't know how he continues to get away with it."

"I can show you when we get to my place."

"How much farther?"

"It's only a few more miles. You're not re-ally going back to that motel, are you?"

"I've already rented the room."

"Did you leave your things there?"

Jamie hated to tell him she'd been afraid to leave her stuff behind for fear someone would break in and steal it. "No, everything I have is in bags behind the seat."

"Would you reconsider staying at my place if I told you there were no strings attached?

And that I'm willing to share what I have regardless of whether you agree to work with me or not?"

"Why would you do that?"

"I keep telling you, I'm a nice guy."

Jamie raised an eyebrow. "And I'm your ticket to get to Harlan?"

"I'll have to admit you look pretty good in that outfit. I keep hoping you'll fall out of that top. And, yes, I think Rawlins noticed."

"Darn right he noticed. As a matter of fact, I'm meeting with him tomorrow to work on my, um, problem."

"No kidding? What's he going to do, ask the good Lord to send down a lightning bolt when you try to enter a shopping center?"

"Not exactly."

Max looked at her. "You're blushing, Jamie. What's up? I can tell when you're keeping something from me."

She would have to tell him the truth sooner or later. "Max, what I told the congregation and what I told Rawlins were two different things."

"I'm listening."

"I had to say something that would get his attention."

"I'm still listening."

"I told him I was a sex addict."

"You did what!"

"It was the only way. How else do you think I managed to get a personal invitation to his home for private counseling?"

Max did not look happy. "Let me get this straight. You're going to Harlan Rawlins's home without backup, *knowing* full well that he's somehow involved with the mob? Not only that, we already know he has a weakness for women, and you've told him you're a sex addict. Great idea, Jamie. Why don't you throw a little meat to a lion while you're at it? Dammit!"

"I wouldn't go if I weren't convinced it was safe. I'm sure he has plenty of staff on hand, not to mention his family."

"You don't know what you're up against. By now Harlan and his mob pals know the man they hired to take me out is dead. The fact that the hit man, Vito Puccini, didn't get the job done will make them even more determined to succeed. They may have already hired someone else to take me out. They could be searching for me at this very moment."

Jamie remained silent.

"The bottom line is we need to work together on this for both of our sakes," Max said.

"So what's it going to take to convince you?"

Jamie knew he had a point, but she wasn't going to give in that easy.

"First, admit that my plan could work."

Max glanced over at her. "I'm not saying it's a bad plan; I'm saying you need backup. You really need to see what I have on Rawlins. Then you'll understand why I feel the way I do."

"OK, I'll see what you've got."

"Take a right at the next road and drive until you see the cabin. There aren't any other houses nearby."

Jamie turned down a dirt road where *No Trespassing* signs made it plain visitors weren't welcome. A minute later, she pulled into a driveway beside a rough-hewn log cabin. She looked around. "Where are the security cameras?"

Max smiled. "You won't find them. You'll know if somebody comes near the property because it'll set off an alarm inside."

"Loud enough to give me heart failure?"

He chuckled. "No, just loud enough so you can hear from any of the rooms."

Jamie climbed from the truck and opened the tailgate so Fleas could jump out. He whizzed on the nearest bush and followed them inside the cabin. It was cool. The scent of wild-flowers rode on a breeze coming through the living room windows. The room had obviously been designed for comfort. The overstuffed sofa and chairs, adorned in a country print, faced a wall-sized stone fireplace. A TV sat in one corner, a bookshelf in the opposite. The room was large and shared space with a kitchen that held an old trestle table made of pine. It was simple and inviting.

"The beds come with feather mattresses," Max said.

"How many bathrooms?"

He hesitated. "There's a half-bath in the loft but only one with a tub, and it's in the hall across from the bedroom where you'd be sleeping. If you decide to stay."

Jamie nodded her approval. "Nice place you got here, Holt."

"Muffin found it while we were still chasing bad guys in Beaumont. From what I under-stand, it was in bad shape. A team of contrac-tors practically rebuilt it from the ground up in less than a week."

"Jeez, I can't get a toilet repaired that fast."

"You do what you have to do."

"Won't people think it strange that the cabin

was repaired almost overnight? What if the contractors talk?"

"They work for me."

"Why am I not surprised?"

"So what do you say? You want to give it a try?"

Jamie pondered it. She had promised herself to stay as far away from Max Holt as possible, but here she was, standing only a few feet from him and wishing she didn't find him so sexy. On the flip side, Jamie knew she needed him for the job at hand. He had the technology and the contacts.

Max smiled. "You're chewing your bottom lip. That means you're considering it."

"We should set a few ground rules."

"You're right. You'll have to stop giving me the come-on."

Her look was deadpan.

He sighed. "What are the rules?"

"We agree to keep this strictly business."

"That depends. Do you plan to walk around in those short skirts and tank tops all the time?"

"Be serious."

"I'm being very serious."

"I have to dress like this when I meet with Harlan. I'm trying to bait him."

"Damn good bait if you ask me. I'd bite."

She tried to ignore him. Yet she couldn't help but admit she derived a certain amount of satisfaction knowing she had captured Max's imagination. "Rule number two: I want to know everything that's going on at all times. No surprises. I'm serious about getting my story, so I have to be able to document everything as it happens. I'll also need to use some of the background information you've gathered on Harlan and the mob."

"Some of the information came from, um, sources that I'm not supposed to know even exist."

"Oh, great. Meaning you and Muffin have been busting through computer firewalls and deciphering codes again."

"Sometimes I break the rules." He saw her look. "Not that I have any intention of breaking the rules you're setting right now, of course."

"Yeah, right."

"And I might enjoy helping you with your story. I happen to know a little bit about the newspaper business if you'll recall."

Jamie was reminded that was one of the reasons he'd been eager to invest in her fledgling newspaper to begin with. Max had worked for his cousin's newspaper, and she had also seen firsthand how savvy he was when it came to what readers liked.

Finally, she shrugged. "I'll listen to suggestions," she said, "as long as you realize I'm not giving you editorial control, and you're not getting a byline."

"You're a hard woman, Jamie. Does this mean you're in?"

"Show me what you've got on Rawlins."

Max handed her a folder.

Jamie sat on the sofa and opened the file. Max took a chair opposite her. After a moment, she looked up. "I'm impressed."

"And so you should be."

"How did you know Rawlins wouldn't be touring at this time?"

"We got lucky. If he'd been on tour we would have come up with a different plan. It just worked out this way."

"I see he actually received his master of divinity from one of the best seminaries in the country."

"With a heavy emphasis on pastoral counseling," Max said. "Which permitted him to take all the psychology courses he wanted. Bottom line: He knows people."

"No wonder he makes such a good shark. Nice photo. Shows off his blue eyes."

"Stop drooling; you're supposed to remain objective, remember?"

"Do you think you could hold off being insufferable until I've had a chance to study Rawlins's file?"

"So you're saying you and me, a hot shower, and me licking you dry afterward isn't likely?"

A shiver ran up Jamie's backbone, touching each vertebra along the way. "See what I mean? I haven't been here five minutes, and you're already breaking the rules."

Max moved to the sofa. His gaze met hers. "You know the score. You knew it when you walked through that front door."

Jamie felt his thigh touch hers, but she refused to move and make a big deal out of it. "What are you trying to say?"

"You're after something."

She arched one brow. "And that something would be you?"

He shrugged. "I know the story is important to you. The fact you might have me as well is just an added bonus."

It was all she could do to keep from bursting into laughter. His sense of humor was one of the qualities she most appreciated in him. "Enjoying yourself, Max?" she said as though talking to a child. It didn't help that Max had already painted a picture in her mind of the two of them naked beneath a warm spray of water.

She took a deep breath and studied the printout before her. Max was quiet, but she could sense his gaze on her, smell his aftershave. She was attracted to him on all levels. But she had to stop thinking along those lines, because she already knew the dangers. Max Holt was hazardous to a woman's heart.

"I see Rawlins's psychology courses helped immensely in his calling," she said, changing the subject. "It says here that he uses a number of techniques to win people over and control his followers."

"Brainwashing, fear tactics, and hypnosis being among them," Max said. "There's also a lot of peer pressure from within the group. People like to fit in. Rawlins plants his people in the group to draw visitors in and keep them in."

Jamie wished Max would scoot over, but to suggest it would let him know he was having an effect on her. Not that he didn't already know, she reminded herself. Max knew women, and he knew how to play them.

"So this is what you wanted me to see."

"I thought it might give you insight as to the kind of man we're dealing with."

"But why would he go to so much trouble when most of this area is impoverished? Why isn't he trying to convert the wealthy?"

"Rawlins knows he isn't going to make money in Sweet Pea, but how would it look to the public if he didn't help the people he grew up with? He's offered to meet their donations tenfold. It might make headlines, but tenfold of almost nothing equals very little out of his pocket. There aren't many people who can afford to give." Max paused. "As for converting the wealthy, Rawlins has managed to snare an impressive number of those with fat wallets. He plays golf, sails, and he's big on charitable events."

"Which means he rubs elbows with the right people."

Max nodded. "And his PR person makes sure Harlan's name is in the newspaper every chance he gets. His notoriety and charm are a big draw to people."

"He's fighting for new industry in this area," Jamie said. "Not only has he donated money from his ministry, he's rallied support from other organizations."

"His ministry appears squeaky clean," Max said. "He presents himself to the world as a happily married man with a two-year-old son he dotes on. You have to know where to look to find the real story."

Jamie held up the papers. "Who would take the time to collect this much information on Rawlins, and why?" When Max didn't answer, she tried to guess. "The FBI, right? They've caught wind of his mob connections."

"Could be."

"You're not going to tell me?"

"You haven't agreed to work with me."

Jamie looked up. "I have a question, Max. Do you believe in miracles? Other than the fact it's a miracle we're still alive after what we've been through?"

"That's one heck of a way to change the subject, but to answer your question, I believe in living by my wits."

"In other words, you can't imagine a power greater than yourself. Why am I not surprised?"

"I didn't say that." He smiled. "I'm glad we're going to be spending a lot of time together here," he said, indicating the cabin. "It's a very intimate setting. We'll have time to work on us."

Jamie rolled her eyes. Talk about changing the subject, but then, Max might be one of those people who kept his beliefs private.

"There is no *us,* Max, except in your own mind."

He looked amused. "I hope you didn't make that date with Rawlins just to make me jealous."

He was back to his old antics. "Would you cut it out?" Finally, Jamie stood and moved to the chair. "By the way, he thinks my name is Jane."

Max chuckled. "Very original. Now you're going to need a last name. How do you like the name Matt Trotter?"

"Why do you ask?"

"It's the name I'm using." He pulled out several cards. "Driver's license, Social Security card, and my employee card from Bennett Electric. Like my picture? I wasn't crazy about my new look at first, but I think it works."

Of course it *worked,* Jamie thought. The truth was, the man would have been handsome with pork chops hanging from his ears. "I take it this new job of yours is just a front?"

"Yeah. I'm really working for an escort service."

"How do you plan to find time to investigate Rawlins and his mob friends?"

"I have a nice boss."

"Meaning money has exchanged hands."

"It happens. Now that you've decided to

sign on with me, so to speak, you'll need identification. I'll snap a picture of the new you,
scan it, and e-mail it to a friend of mine. Next
time you walk out that door, you'll have a
brand-new identity."

"Oh, yeah? Who am I supposed to be?"

"Jane Trotter. My wife."

FIVE

"WE'RE SUPPOSED TO BE MARRIED?" JAMIE blurted in disbelief.

"Can you think of a better explanation as to why we're sharing a cabin in the woods?"

"Why can't we be brother and sister?"

Max shook his head. "Jamie, Jamie, Jamie. Someone would notice how you look at me, and our cover would be blown."

She did a massive eye roll. "Oh, puh-lease."

"Face it, Swifty: You have lust in your eyes, and it has my name written all over it."

"You know, I've discovered the best way to deal with you is to ignore most of what you say. Frankly, I don't see why we have to explain anything."

"We're going to try and infiltrate the good

reverend's ministry, sweetheart. Hopefully, we'll meet some of the key players. Who knows? One of us might end up teaching Sunday school."

"Harlan might be discouraged if I tell him I'm married."

"Actually, it works to his benefit. The last thing he wants to deal with is a messy entanglement. You can pretend you're trying to curb your, uh, addiction in order to save your marriage. You're not really going to have sex with him. . . ." Max paused.

"What?" Jamie said when he didn't finish. She frowned. "You're not afraid something is going to happen between Harlan and me. You're not thinking—"

"I don't know what to think," Max said. "What if you get cornered? What if he forces himself on you?" Max shook his head. "I'll have to level with you, Jamie. I've felt uneasy about the man from the beginning. We don't know what he's capable of."

It was as if a lightbulb suddenly went off in Jamie's head. "So *that's* why you changed your mind about bringing me along," she said, remembering Max's change of heart had come after Muffin had told them about Rawlins's history with women.

Max hesitated. "I knew you would try to think of a way to play him, that you would place yourself right in the line of fire, so to speak. And I was right. You showed up in an outfit that was designed to give a man a . . ." He paused. "You get my point."

"Uh, yeah."

"All I'm asking is that you practice a great deal of caution. It's OK to dangle a carrot in front of Rawlins, but it's not OK to take unnecessary chances. When you visit him, Dave and I need to be close by."

"How?"

"Let us worry about that."

"Just don't blow my cover, OK? I spent a lot of money on this wig."

"Wait a minute, Jamie. I don't care if we all blow our covers if Rawlins gets crazy with you. If he tries to use force, Dave and I are going to be on him. That's why you have to agree to work with us as a team. I'm not going to back off on this one, Swifty. You have to agree to that up front."

She sighed. "OK, Max."

"There are ways you might be able to get away without blowing our cover. You can try those first."

"What are they?"

"Having a husband in the wings is one of them. You can tell Harlan any number of things if it looks like the situation is getting out of hand. Tell him your husband is insanely jealous, that you suspect you're being followed. Tell him whatever the hell you have to in order to protect yourself. You could suddenly start feeling guilty. Whatever it takes to stay safe. But if it doesn't work, you scream, you run, you do what you have to do to protect yourself. Dave and I will be close by."

Jamie knew Max was right. "OK," she said. "Husband and wife. We'll need wedding rings."

"I'll take care of it." He suddenly smiled. "So, what do you say? Think we can work together?"

"That depends. Would you promise not to try to disarm any more bombs in my presence?"

"If you'll promise not to be so disagreeable."

"I am *not* disagreeable."

"And we need to discuss the dog."

They both looked at Fleas, who was napping near Jamie's feet. "He stays," she said. "It's a package deal."

Max didn't look happy.

"I'll take care of him. I've already bought everything he needs."

Max studied the lanky bloodhound. "What happened to his hair?"

"Fleas was attacked by a raccoon."

"You're going to allow an animal named Fleas to sleep under the same roof with us?"

"He doesn't have fleas. It's his *name*. Obviously somebody thought it was funny. Besides, we need a good watchdog."

"And that would be him?"

"Of course. He's very alert when he isn't sleeping. I think he's already attached to me. I can't even take a shower without him following me into the bathroom."

"Oh, now you've done it," Max said. "You've gone and turned me on." He grinned.

"Trust me, you're perfectly capable of doing it to yourself." Jamie glanced around. "Is there anything to eat in this place? I'm starving."

"I can scramble some eggs. I'm great with scrambled eggs." Max got up.

"Sounds good to me," Jamie replied, jumping to her feet as well. "I need to grab Fleas's food from the truck."

"I'll go with you. We can grab the rest of your things while we're at it."

"I don't have much. I left my suitcase in your car."

"I've already brought it in."

"Where *is* your car, by the way?" Jamie asked, standing in the doorway, looking across the yard.

"In the garage. Remind me to give you the security code for the garage and the cabin before we go to bed."

Jamie opened the door to her truck and reached behind the seat for the bags she'd stuffed behind it. One held her new underwear and toiletry items, the other her dirty clothes, and a separate bag held Fleas's dry dog food and bowls. She made a note to buy more slut-wear.

"By the way, how is Muffin?" she asked once they started back toward the cabin. As odd as it sounded even to her, she had missed Max's computer.

Max opened the door and waited for Jamie to enter. "She's not very happy with me at the moment, thanks to you."

"What did I do?"

"You refused to get back in my car. You just took off on us." Max closed the door after them and locked it, then punched a series of numbers on an alarm panel. "Naturally Muffin missed you and was worried."

Jamie would not have thought Muffin capable of feeling emotions had she not witnessed it for herself. Muffin also had attitude. She did not mind telling Max where he could get off. Jamie had liked her right away. And to think, she had doubted Max the first time he'd told her about his computer; in fact, she had thought him crazy. Hell, she had doubted her own sanity in her earlier conversations with Muffin. Now, as strange as it sounded, Muffin felt like an old friend.

"And you weren't worried about me that I took off?" Jamie asked.

Max shrugged. "I knew you could handle yourself."

They stood there for a moment, simply looking at each other. Jamie studied the handsome olive-skinned face, gazing into those dark eyes that seemed as if they had been created to turn a woman's stomach to mush. She had run her fingers through his hair. She had kissed those delicious lips, tasted him, run her fingers along the strong stubborn jaw.

She knew he was attracted to her, he'd said it plenty of times, and she supposed he cared about her to an extent, but neither of them was clear about their feelings after only two weeks of knowing each other.

Not that it had been an ordinary two weeks, she reminded herself, and she *had* been engaged to another man during that time. Still, they had come mighty close to having sex one night—and it had been a night Jamie would never forget. Max had never mentioned it, but Jamie knew she, for one, was still thinking about it.

Now, as he gazed back at her, Jamie wished she knew what he was thinking. Max was not one who shared his thoughts easily. Sure, he'd made it plain more than once that he would have enjoyed a rumble beneath the sheets, but where his feelings were concerned he was about as close-mouthed as they came.

"Hey, you're awfully quiet," Max said. "Is something wrong?"

Jamie gave an inward sigh. By meeting up with Max she had once again placed her heart in a precarious position. "I'm just tired. Maybe you could show me where I'm sleeping."

"Right this way."

She followed him down a short hall. He paused at the door, reached inside, and flipped on the light, then motioned her into the room as he set her bags down. "The bathroom is right across the hall. While you get situated, I'll start the eggs."

"Thanks."

Jamie stepped into the bedroom and sat on the old four-poster bed, testing the mattress. Max was right; it was stuffed with feathers. She could do some serious sleeping on this bed. A cool breeze rustled the curtains and fell softly on her skin. Jamie suddenly felt more relaxed than she had in days.

She glanced at the oak dresser against the wall and frowned at the woman in the mirror. She pulled off the wig, unpinned her blonde hair, and finger-combed it. Much better, she thought. Now she only had to scrape off an inch-thick layer of makeup.

Jamie could hear Max cracking the eggs into a bowl in the kitchen as she crossed the hall to the bathroom. She grinned at the old claw-foot bathtub and imagined herself sitting inside it with bubbles up to her ears. A metal hoop had been positioned over the tub, hanging from it a floral shower curtain. A porcelain sink was perched on one wall; someone had attached a skirt to it that matched both the shower and the window curtain. A wicker basket beside the tub was stuffed with fluffy bath towels.

Max was in the process of chopping green

peppers on an old-fashioned butcher block when Jamie entered the kitchen for her suitcase. "I thought you were just going to scramble a few eggs," she said, peering over his shoulder. "I should help."

He turned and held his hands out, blocking her. "Actually, I don't permit anyone in the kitchen when I'm preparing my secret recipe."

"Why is it a secret?"

"Because of all the special ingredients that go into it. Why don't you just rest for a few minutes?"

Jamie noticed Fleas standing beside Max as though waiting for something. "Have you been feeding my dog?"

"I gave him a little cheese. Dogs like cheese."

"He should be eating real dog food." Jamie pulled his food and dog dishes from a bag.

"I'll feed him," Max said. "Just go back to what you were doing. Oh, I wrote down the alarm code. It's on the table."

"OK, I'll get out of your way, but don't give Fleas any more cheese. He'll get fat."

Jamie grabbed her suitcase and returned to her room. Inside she found her favorite cutoff jeans. She stepped out of her short skirt and high heels and pulled them on. She unpacked her bag, put her newly purchased shampoo, toothbrush, and toothpaste inside the bathroom cabinet, and hurried back into the kitchen, where she found Max, scooping eggs onto plates.

"That looks wonderful," she said, noting that Max had added ham, onions, and cheese to the eggs. He'd even made toast. Jamie grabbed napkins and flatware and went about setting the table as Max poured orange juice.

"This is good," Jamie said after tasting her food.

"My cousin Nick taught me how to run a newspaper; his wife Billie taught me how to cook." Max looked up from his food. "I've always wanted to take a gourmet cooking class."

"Why haven't you?"

"My schedule doesn't really permit it."

"Who takes care of your horse farm in Virginia while you're away?"

"I have a guy who looks after things. He's been with me for years now."

"Don't you miss being home?"

"Yeah. I'll probably go back for a while once I'm done here."

"Isn't Holt Industries based there?"

"Uh-huh. I have offices in other locations,

but the home office is in Loudoun County, Virginia."

"And what do you do in those offices?"

Max regarded her. "Mostly technological research, but I've expanded over the years. We're doing some biomedical research, and I'm putting out bids soon to build a lab to study viruses."

"Isn't that already being done?"

"Not fast enough."

"You're amazing," Jamie said.

"Yeah?"

"You've got your fingers in everything."

"Keeps boredom at bay."

"But you could afford to retire anytime you like."

"What would I do, Jamie?"

She laughed. "With your money? Any damn thing you wanted. You could travel the world."

"I already have. Several times."

"Isn't there anything you haven't done?"

Max sat back in his chair and looked thoughtful. "Until today I'd never ridden in a pickup truck with a redhead and a hound dog."

"Seriously, Max."

"If you could retire tomorrow, would you?"

Jamie hesitated. "I'd probably still want to write a few articles. It's sort of in my blood."

"You'll never stop working, Jamie. You're too much like me. When you do what you love, it never feels like work. That doesn't mean I don't like to take off and play. I'm big on vacations. But I need direction. A reason for being."

"Your marriage to Bunny didn't provide that?" She tried to hide her smile.

Max scowled. "That was *not* her real name. And no, the marriage was all wrong from the start."

"Why'd you marry her?"

"Because I was dumb and infatuated. End of story."

"Do you wish you'd had children with her?"

"Why are you asking these questions? You're beginning to sound like Muffin."

"I was merely trying to carry on polite conversation, Max. I certainly didn't mean to intrude."

"I don't question you about your love life." He bit off a piece of toast and chewed. "She was not an airhead. People just assumed she was because of the way she looked."

"The way she looked?"

"Well, hell, Jamie, the woman was . . ." Max paused.

"Gorgeous," Jamie said.

"Yeah, and she had this—"

"Great body," Jamie interrupted.

"Uh-huh."

Jamie dropped her fork, and it clattered loudly. "Well, now isn't that special."

"I thought so in the beginning."

Jamie stood and picked up her plate.

"What are you doing?" Max asked. "You haven't finished eating."

"I'm not hungry."

"You were starving a few minutes ago."

Jamie raked her eggs into Fleas's bowl, and the dog dived on it. "I'm really very tired."

Max chuckled. "You mean you're really very jealous."

Jamie cut her eyes at him. "I am not jealous. I just don't want to talk about your ex-wife's body."

"Hey, you're the one who brought it up."

Fleas finished eating and gazed at Max's plate.

Max stood. "You're saying you've never noticed a man's body?"

"I notice a man's eyes first."

"Uh-huh."

"But I've dated some very fit men, Max."

"You want to see fit?" Max suddenly lifted

his shirt, exposing a flat, hair-roughened stomach. "Feel that."

Jamie decided her first mistake was looking. Oh God. He had one of those hard washboard stomachs that she'd only heard women talk about. And that hair, the way it fanned out so nicely across his stomach, the way it whorled around his navel and— She dropped her gaze, found herself suddenly staring at his zipper. Oh God, oh God, oh God. It didn't help that his unshaved jaw made him even more appealing.

Max grabbed Jamie's wrist and pressed her hand against his abdomen.

Skin touched skin.

"It's hard as a rock," he said proudly. "Not an ounce of flab anywhere."

Jamie swallowed. Felt like a giant turnip was trying to make its way down her windpipe. Felt like something had cut off her breath and she was going to have to use the Heimlich maneuver on herself in order to get air.

She jerked her hand free. "Would you cut that out!"

"I was trying to make a point." Max pulled his shirt down, grabbed his plate, and raked his food into Fleas's bowl. The dog scrambled toward it.

"He's not supposed to be eating that," Jamie said.

"You fed him yours."

"I decided to give him a little treat. I don't want him to get used to eating people food on account it isn't good for him. I'm going to bed. Come on, Fleas, let's go."

"You're letting him sleep in your room? Man, that's one lucky dog."

Jamie ignored him.

Fleas wolfed down the remaining food before following Jamie into her bedroom. She closed the door and locked it. "I know what you're thinking," she said. "You're thinking I didn't handle that very well."

He belched in response.

JAMIE WAITED UNTIL MAX WENT TO BED BEfore going out to his car. She needed a friend, and Muffin, despite being a computer, was the closest thing she had at the moment.

She punched a set of numbers into the alarm panel, hit a button, and the garage door rose automatically. She hurried inside and yanked open the car door.

"Hey, Muffin, it's me," she said once she'd climbed into the car.

"Jamie, don't you *ever* sneak up on me like that again! I almost hit the panic button."

"This place has too many alarms," Jamie grumbled. "I can't go to the bathroom without fear of setting something off."

"What are you doing here?" Muffin asked. "I thought you'd gone back to Beaumont."

"I decided to come to Tennessee on my own," she said. "You know how badly I want to do a story on Harlan Rawlins and his mob buddies. So, I said to hell with Max and came on my own."

"Where are you staying?"

"With Max."

"Oh." Muffin paused. "Did I miss something?"

Jamie filled her in on all that had happened since her arrival.

"You actually went to Harlan's church and told him you were a sex addict?" Muffin said in disbelief.

"Yep. After all, you're the one who told me he had a weakness for women. You should have seen the look on his face. I'm meeting him tomorrow for private counseling. I wish you could see me, Muffin. I look like I'm peddling poontang, for sure." Jamie laughed. It was good talking to Muffin again. And easy to forget she was a voice-activated computer.

"It sounds dangerous to me, kiddo. What does Max have to say about this?"

"He wasn't exactly thrilled to see me at church, but we got past that. By the way, Max and I are supposed to be married."

"Oh God, this'll never work."

"It has to, Muffin. This is the chance I've been waiting for. My big break. And it's only the beginning."

"Listen, Jamie, you don't know what you're getting into. This Rawlins guy could be dangerous. Especially if he's in tight with the mob like we think he is."

"OK, if I sound like I'm not taking it seriously it's because I'm excited. But I'm very much aware of the risks. I'm not leaving anything to chance. It's not like Max and I haven't faced danger before."

"The two of you were very lucky to get out of Beaumont alive," Muffin said. "You can't afford to take chances now."

"I promise I'll be careful. Look, I have to get back to the house in case Max wakes up. Don't tell him I talked to you. Try to act surprised when he tells you I'm back."

Muffin sighed. "I knew this was going to get complicated."

MAX TOSSED IN HIS BED FOR AN HOUR BEFORE he climbed out and pulled on his jeans. He slipped from the house quietly. A moment later he was telling Muffin all that had taken place since they'd last talked.

"Jamie just blew into town in an old pickup truck with an ugly bloodhound in the back," he said. "I couldn't let her go after Rawlins on her own, so I convinced her to work with me. She's staying at my cabin."

"How are the two of you getting along?"

"Jamie promised not to be difficult."

"And what did you promise?"

Max sounded defensive when he spoke. "Are you saying I'm difficult?"

"Now where would I get an idea like that?"

"OK," he said begrudgingly. "I promised not to disable any more bombs. You got anything for me?" he asked, stifling a yawn.

"I'm still working on it. Have you and Dave finalized your plans?"

"Yeah, but then Jamie showed up and that changed everything."

"You have to admire her spunk."

"Yeah, I guess. I just hope she doesn't get us all killed."

SIX

Jamie shivered as something wet and moist nuzzled her ear. "Cut it out, Max." She pulled the bed pillow over her head and sank farther into the feather mattress. The pillow shifted. She was jolted fully awake, this time by a wet tongue at the back of her neck. Her scalp tingled and she could feel the goose pimples on her arm. She shouted in irritation, "Max, I said stop it!" She yanked the pillow aside as Fleas skittered beneath the tall bed, toenails clicking across the old plank floors.

"Oh, damn," she muttered. "I must've had another X-rated dream about Max."

Coming off the bed, Jamie dropped to her knees and peered beneath it. "I'm sorry, boy. I thought you were this pervert I know." She offered her hand. Fleas sniffed once and thumped his tail in response.

"Come on out. I won't hurt you."

The dog hesitated and then crawled from beneath the bed. Jamie regarded him. His folds seemed more prominent this morning. "Jeez, pal, a little collagen in those wrinkles would work wonders, you know."

The dog cocked his head to one side. His skin seemed to slide with the motion. Jamie shook her head sadly and glanced about the small bedroom. She was still tired. After her visit with Muffin she'd lain awake for a good two hours, finally falling asleep around 2:00 A.M. She gave a wide unladylike yawn.

"Have you seen Max?" she asked Fleas. "You remember him, the guy with the hard stomach? The one who kinda looks like something you'd find in a Calvin Klein ad? Like someone you'd want to share a hot tub with?"

Jamie sighed. First she'd had a sexy dream; now she was thinking about Max's body. And she hadn't even had her first cup of coffee. Well, it was all his fault; he'd started it by lifting up his shirt.

"Watch yourself, kiddo," she told herself, "or you'll end up falling for him all over again."

Falling for him? Uh-oh. The thought shocked her. No, no, she wasn't falling for him; she was simply attracted to him, that's all. What woman wouldn't be? Looking into those sexy eyes of his was almost like having foreplay with him, for Pete's sake! Damn him for making her think things she had no right thinking.

The dog made a sound. "What is it?" Jamie asked. Finally, it hit her. "Oh, I'll bet you have to go to the bathroom. Oh, hell, Fleas, I knew I'd make a terrible pet owner. And you know it, too, don't you? That's why you look so sad."

Jamie sighed and walked from the room in her nightshirt, the lanky bloodhound on her heels. She let him out the front door. "How about sniffing out the nearest Dunkin' Donuts while you're at it?"

She checked her wristwatch while she waited for him to do his business. Six o'clock. No wonder she was so tired. She was the kind of person who needed eight hours of sleep or she became disagreeable, as Max sometimes accused.

Fleas returned and Jamie closed the door behind them. She wondered what Max was up to. She glanced toward the loft, which she assumed held another bed. "Max, are you up?"

No answer.

"He's probably in his car talking to his computer," she told the dog. "You don't know about Max's computer. Her name is Muffin, and she's capable of doing just about anything. Maybe she can find you a nice plastic surgeon."

The dog thumped his tail against the floor.

"Maybe she can find me a shrink. I talk to computers; I talk to dogs." Fleas looked at his bowl. "Oh, yeah, it's time to feed you. See, I'm not very reliable; you have to remind me of these things." She grabbed the sack of dry food and shook some into his dish. "Breakfast is served," she announced.

Fleas simply blinked back at her. "Listen to me, pal: This is primo dog food. It's supposed to keep you fit and trim and give you all the vitamins you need." He responded by slumping to the floor. "OK, so you're not a breakfast dog. I usually like to have a couple of cups of coffee myself before I eat. Sometimes I don't even bother with breakfast. Saves calories. That way I can pile up on junk food later. I shouldn't be telling you this on account I need to set a good example for you."

Jamie found the automatic coffeemaker and

filled a cup. She sat down at the old pine table and looked about. She felt lost and disoriented, and she suspected it was due to lack of sleep mixed with anxiety mixed with wondering how she and Max would live under the same roof for the next few days.

She forced the thought aside, turning her attention to the appointment she had with Harlan Rawlins in less than six hours. She had to admit she was worried; indeed, she could find herself in a compromising position if she weren't careful. She would have to stay one step ahead of him at all times.

Jamie hurried into her bedroom for the notepad she'd purchased on her shopping trip. As she sipped her coffee, she jotted down her first impressions of Harlan.

"Handsome and charismatic," she wrote. "A man who knows how to work a crowd," she added, scribbling quickly. She'd devised her own form of shorthand long ago from interviewing people. She continued writing. Harlan Rawlins seemed sincere when it came to the less fortunate, but his weakness for women and his ties to the mob told a different story.

Jamie paused and clicked the pen against her bottom teeth, something Vera often got on her for doing. Lord, Vera was going to skin her alive when she got back to Beaumont. She thought of the woman who had been the next best thing to a mother when Jamie's biological mother had left while she was still in diapers. Vera, who had always been there for her.

Vera had taught her to be strong and to meet challenges head-on. As a result, she had refused to give up on the newspaper. She had sold almost everything she owned in order to keep it afloat, and she had swallowed her pride when an investor had offered to help her out. That investor had been Max Holt, of course. Max bailed her out and put a large chunk of change in an account so Jamie would never have to struggle again.

Jamie looked forward to the day she could pay him back. It might sound like a grand plan at this point, but she was determined.

Guilt hit her as soon as she thought of Vera. She had no right to cause the woman to worry. With a heavy sigh, Jamie put down her pen and grabbed the portable phone from the kitchen counter. She had a choice. She could call Vera at home and listen to the woman rant and rave or she could call the newspaper office, knowing Vera wouldn't be in at this hour, and leave a message.

Jamie dialed the office. "Hello, Vera, it's me," she said, trying to make her voice light and airy, as though she were having the time of her life. "Just wanted to let you know I'm enjoying my little vacation and I'm resting. I'm going to have a great story when I get back. I'll call again soon, please don't worry about me." She hung up and regarded Fleas.

"See that? Here I am, a grown woman, and I still have to check in. That's because I've always done the responsible thing until I met Max. I was a lot more stable and hardly ever thought about sex before he came into my life and turned it topsy-turvy.

"See, I like predictability. I like having a routine." Like drinking her coffee in her favorite mug with the big smiley face on it, she thought. And sitting in her favorite chair when she watched the news on TV. Simple things that brought her pleasure. She preferred Dove soap to the store brand because one of her earliest memories made her think of that smell.

Could it have been her mother? she'd asked herself a hundred times. She doubted it, since her mother, as best Jamie could determine, had left when Jamie was about two years old. Perhaps she had dreamed it. What she *did* remember, as though it had been yesterday, was snooping through a box in the attic that had held her mother's few belongings and finding a bar of Dove soap inside. She'd hidden it in her underwear drawer, taking it out occasionally so she could sniff its clean scent.

Even now, she kept a bar on her night table because she liked turning over in the middle of the night and smelling its fragrance, and it was all she ever bathed in. She still had the old bar tucked inside her lingerie drawer. And as silly as it sounded, she was annoyed that she had forgotten to buy it at the store the previous day.

Jamie's stomach growled. She crossed the kitchen and grabbed a cookie from a jar that had been painted with roosters and matched the set of canisters nearby. The coffee was not doing what it was supposed to do, namely, wake her up. Where the heck was Max? She climbed the narrow steps that led to the loft area.

The bed was empty and unmade. Jamie slid her hand across the smooth sheet. The pillow bore the imprint of Max's head and the subtle scent of his aftershave. She plucked a dark hair from it and tried not to imagine Max warm and naked beneath the old quilt.

Here we go again, she thought.

What was wrong with her? She was lusting after a man, that's what. Her hormones must be out of whack. Or maybe her defenses were down due to fatigue.

She stared at the empty bed. It looked so inviting. Perhaps if she just closed her eyes for fifteen minutes. She lay down on the soft mattress, nuzzled her face into Max's pillow, and drifted off to sleep.

SEVEN

HARLAN RAWLINS SMOOTHED HIS HAND OVER his perfect blonde hair and readjusted his tie. His white dress shirt was European-cut. It fit nicely against his well-toned body and brought out his tan, both of which he worked hard to keep, even when he was on the road. One of the 18-wheeler trucks that carried Love Ministry's tents and other equipment also contained a gym, complete with a portable hot tub and tanning bed.

His entourage included a personal trainer and masseuse, a chef who saw that Harlan maintained a healthy but delicious eating regimen, and a publicist and PR person who purchased licenses and permits for the ministry, contacted the newspapers and TV and radio stations, and set up news conferences.

Harlan's administrative assistant saw that Harlan stayed on schedule and had exactly what he needed at all times, and even wrote some of Harlan's speeches and sermons. A personal valet saw to Harlan's extensive wardrobe, shaved him, trimmed his hair, gave him manicures, pedicures, and facials, and made sure the minister's personal belongings were laid out upon his arrival. A bodyguard traveled with Harlan and was responsible for arranging for the female "guests" who visited Harlan's hotel rooms from time to time.

Now, sitting at his desk in his private office, Harlan spoke to the woman on the other end of the line, using the voice that inspired confidence and had brought many to salvation. Only this morning it was marked with fatigue and had a certain edge to it. He cradled the phone between his shoulder and jaw, freeing his hands so that he could massage his temples where a headache had been brewing for the last hour. His forehead was damp.

"Honey, I've only been back three days. Of course I was going to call you, but my little boy has a nasty summer cold and I've been spending time with him. You know I can't count on his mama to see to his care, what with her emotional problems." Suddenly he lost his connection. The lights flickered in his office, not for the first time. He looked up and frowned.

Someone knocked on his door. "Yes?" he called out.

His bodyguard, Ward Reed, peeked inside. He was a tall, angular man with hard eyes and thin lips. Not only did he accompany Harlan wherever the minister went; he saw to home security as well. "Mr. Santoni is here."

Harlan froze. *"Here?* What's he doing *here?"*

"I know we've discouraged him from coming to your home in the past, but I suggest we go ahead and let him in this time. I want to know what's so important that he decided to show up at your front door so early in the day."

Harlan sighed. "Greed, what else? I don't like this, Ward." He wiped his brow. "What's wrong with the power? The lights are flashing on and off and the phone just died on me."

"We've got electrical problems. I've already reported it, but it'll take a while for the men to get here. May lose power for a while; the generator will eventually kick in." As if acting on cue, the lights flickered, and the office went dark.

"Just what I need," Harlan said. "I want to meet with a man like Santoni in a dark office."

Ward pulled a cord and the drapes whispered open. July sunlight filled the room. "I'll be here the whole time." He studied the man. "You don't look so good."

"I didn't sleep last night. My mind was racing ninety miles an hour."

"You can't keep this up, Harlan. You look strung out, man."

"You know what touring does to me."

"Yeah, but you're taking way too much medication. You have to take something to make you sleep, something to keep you awake. You need to see a doctor."

"Let Santoni in," Harlan interrupted.

Ward gave the man a long, hard look. Finally, he shrugged. "Whatever you say."

Nick Santoni stepped through the door a moment later with Ward Reed on his heels. Santoni wore a soft dove gray suit that had been shipped directly from Milan, the likes of which could not be purchased in a town like Sweet Pea or Knoxville for any amount. His black hair was perfect.

"Well, well, the lamb of God has returned

to his holy mansion on the mountain." He glanced around the dark room. "Did you forget to pay your electric bill?"

Harlan offered him a tight smile. "We're having problems with the power. Were we supposed to meet today, Mr. Santoni? I don't have you listed in my appointment book."

Nick smiled and held out his arms in greeting. "What's this 'Mr. Santoni' business?" he asked. "How many times have I asked you to call me Nick? I like to think we're not only business associates but friends as well. Surely you can spare a few minutes of your time."

"Of course." Harlan's voice trembled.

"By the way, your home is lovely. I had no idea ministers lived so well. You've even got marble pillars in the foyer. I thought you Christians were supposed to store your treasures in heaven." He paused and winked. "Looks like you couldn't wait, buddy."

"What can I do for you?" Harlan asked. He reached for a tissue, mopped his upper lip.

Nick took a chair across from Harlan's desk. Reed sat on the sofa against the wall. "I wish I had good news, my friend," Nick began, "but the family has been putting pressure on me to up your percentage, despite my best efforts to convince them otherwise."

Harlan looked confused. "But we agreed on a cap. We have a gentlemen's agreement."

"Yes, and the Santoni family has always been honorable people, but your situation has changed. Your celebrity status has grown by leaps and bounds in the past few years." He paused. "I'd like to think I am somewhat responsible for your success."

Harlan remained quiet.

"Unfortunately, your fame puts you at a higher risk, and at your current installment, I can't guarantee your protection outside of this state. You could be in serious danger."

Harlan and Reed exchanged looks. "My expenses are already sky-high," Harlan said.

"We're only talking another five percent. I know it sounds like a lot, and I'm very sympathetic to your situation, but my uncle feels strongly about this. There's no changing his mind," Nick added softly.

Harlan pressed his fingertips against his temples but still said nothing.

Nick waited, absently stroking the thin scar that ran from his left eyebrow to his cheekbone, one he'd earned as a wet-behind-the-ears thug who'd gone up against a Jersey gang leader. The surgeon hadn't finished stitching Nick's cut before a jogger found the other man's body in a ditch on the side of a road.

Nevertheless, the scar, while it added a slightly harder edge to Nick's good looks, did not detract from them, and he turned his share of women's heads. Having been groomed for years to be the head of the Santoni family, Nick was polished and carried himself well. He'd lost most of the Jersey accent; he spoke slowly and deliberately and made each word count. He had the look of a banker or corporate attorney.

"You don't look well, Harlan," Nick said.

Harlan rolled his shoulders. "It was a long trip. I ran out of medicine."

Nick reached inside his jacket. He pulled out a small plastic bottle of pills. "Catch." He tossed the bottle, and Harlan lunged at it.

"It'll take the edge off," Nick said, "until I send over the other. I've told you before there is no reason for you to suffer needlessly when I'm only too happy to help."

The lights came on. Harlan straightened in his chair. "I have cooperated with the Santoni family in the past, but this, er, request is unreasonable."

"Now, Harlan," Nick said gently. "The last thing we want to do is create hard feelings between us. The family has always had your best interests at heart."

"We lost the TV network deal," Harlan said. "That was inexcusable."

Nick looked surprised. "Inexcusable? That's a harsh word to use between friends, but then, I know you're not yourself today. The deal simply didn't pan out."

"My portion of the money has not been returned," Harlan said.

Nick looked thoughtful. "Has it not occurred to you that we may have even greater aspirations for you?" he asked. "It would benefit you greatly if you'd learn to become more patient with us. Take the pill, Harlan."

Reed stood and walked over to a cabinet where he poured water into a glass. He handed it to Harlan before facing Nick. "Maybe we could discuss this another time."

"What is there to discuss?" Harlan said. "I can't afford to run a ministry at this rate." He looked at Nick. "Don't you people realize that every time you up your share you take food or medicine away from those who desperately need it? Should I close down all of my outreach programs so the Santoni family can keep getting richer?"

Nick smiled, but it didn't reach his dark

eyes. "This coming from a man who lives like he has already passed through heaven's gate?"

Harlan wiped one hand down his face. Finally, he uncapped the bottle, pulled out the tiny pill, and popped it into his mouth. He didn't bother with the water. "I may as well fold up my tents and retire."

The smile on Nick's face faded. "That would be a mistake, Harlan. You're only talking like that because you don't feel well."

"Is there anything else, Mr. Santoni?" Reed said.

Nick nodded. "Yes, and this should be of concern to all of us. Vito Puccini is dead. He did not do the job for which he was hired. Maximillian Holt is still alive."

"I don't want to hear this," Harlan said. "I had nothing to do with it. The less I know the better. In case the police question me."

"The police will never make a connection," Nick said, "but Maximillian Holt will. He's got a reputation for being very cunning; he has contacts that even we don't have." He paused. "And he has disappeared."

"What do you mean he has disappeared?" Reed asked.

"He's no longer in Beaumont, South Carolina."

"Maybe he got scared," Harlan said. "He could have left the country," he added hopefully. "Heaven knows he can afford to live anywhere in the world he likes."

Nick shook his head. "Max Holt is not the type of man to run. In fact, he could be looking for us as we speak."

"Do you know something we don't?" Reed asked, as though sensing there was more.

"I did not hire Vito whatever-his-name-is, and I'm not going to get involved in this sort of thing," Harlan said.

"Relax, Harlan," Nick said. "That's why you pay us. I just want you to be aware of the problem, that's all." When Harlan continued to look concerned, Nick smiled. "Haven't we always taken care of your problems in the past? Better still, we keep your dirty little secrets."

Harlan started to respond when the door opened and a young boy peeked through. He had Harlan's blonde hair. "Daddy play?" the boy asked.

Harlan literally bolted from his chair, grabbed the boy, and stepped outside the door, where his wife raced down the stairs, eyes bright with fear.

"I'm sorry, Harlan. I turned my back for one minute and he—"

Harlan didn't give her a chance to finish. He slapped her hard across the face. She cried out, at the same time using one arm to fend off another blow.

Harlan's voice was hard as he regarded his wife. "You only have one job in this house, Sarah," he said. "If you can't do it I'll find somebody who can."

The housekeeper joined them in the hall. "Shall I take Harlan Jr.?" she asked.

The lights flickered and came on; the generator had kicked in. Harlan paid scant notice as he passed the boy to his housekeeper. "Watch him closely." He turned to his wife. "You will spend the rest of the day in your room, Sarah, and you will not see my son until tomorrow." He looked at the housekeeper. "Is that clear?"

The woman nodded stiffly. "Of course, Reverend." She carried the boy away.

Nick waited until Harlan took a seat behind his desk before he spoke. "Nice-looking son you have there," he said. "The spitting image of his daddy. I'll bet he idolizes you."

Harlan's jaw grew rigid.

"Oh, look at the time," Nick said. "I fear I've overstayed my welcome." He got up slowly and made for the door. "Call me later,

Harlan. Once you've had time to think about our discussion." He winked. "Oh, and I'll send somebody over later with something to help you sleep tonight. Something a little stronger this time."

EIGHT

WHEN JAMIE OPENED HER EYES SHE FOUND Max staring down at her. She sat upright on the bed, dragging a sheet to her breasts. "What are you doing?"

Max smiled. "Looking at you."

"How long have you been standing there?"

"Long enough to know you got the cutest behind I've ever seen."

Jamie snatched the sheet to her chin. "Don't you have anything better to do than ogle me in my sleep, Holt?"

"I was also thinking how peaceful you look when your eyes are closed and your mouth isn't moving. I could get accustomed to your quiet side. And finding you in my bed."

"Where have you been?"

"Taking care of business."

"Which means you're up to something. I know you." She got up and took the steps down. He followed. The clock in the kitchen pointed to eight o'clock.

"You hungry?" Max asked. "I grabbed a box of fresh donuts from the grocery store while I was out. You know how you like donuts."

Donuts. Damn. The man obviously knew how to work her. "I think I'll shower first," she said, hoping to show some self-control. Max grinned, and she knew she'd failed. "Just don't eat them all."

"You might need this." Max reached into one of the grocery sacks and tossed her a bar of soap.

Jamie was surprised to find a bar of scented Dove soap in her hand. She looked at him. "How did you know?"

"I've spent a lot of time in the car with you; I know your scent. I took a whiff of every bar on the shelf, and this is as close as I came. Was I right?"

Jamie was touched. She couldn't imagine a man like Max taking the time to smell every bar of soap in the store in order to find her brand. "Gee, Max, that was really nice of you."

"I keep telling you I'm a nice guy."

"You can be."

Max smiled as she walked away, her shirt barely concealing her behind.

Jamie showered and changed into cutoff jeans and a tank top. Max had already downed two donuts, but that still left her plenty. She peered into the open box. "Oh, there is a God." She started to reach for a vanilla-glazed donut with bright colorful sprinkles, then paused.

"Come on, Swifty, go for the chocolate-covered one," Max said. "You know you want it."

Jamie grabbed it. She took a bite and closed her eyes. "Yum." She opened her eyes and found Max staring. "What?"

"I like donuts, but I'm not sure I like them that much."

"OK, so you know my weakness."

"By the way, I prefer you as a blonde."

"You and me both. But the red wig is a good disguise." She sighed. "The things I do to keep from getting shot."

Fleas came up beside her and sniffed.

"Forget it, pal," Max told the dog. "You've got a better chance of getting a lung." He reached for a brown envelope and dumped the contents on the table. "Your new identification and—" He pulled two wedding bands from his shirt pocket. "Your ring."

"What? No diamonds?"

"Remember, the idea is to blend. This is not a wealthy area."

Jamie slipped the ring on her finger. "Perfect fit; how did you know?" He shrugged. She glanced at her new driver's license and other identification. "You took this picture of me late last night. How were you able to get all this back so quickly?"

"I asked nicely."

"I'm beginning to think you might have mob connections, too."

"Now, about the truck."

Jamie tossed the last bit of donut into her mouth and licked her fingers. "My truck?"

"Some men are arriving later today to install Muffin into the dashboard. After your appointment with Rawlins," he added. "Nobody will be able to detect the system."

Jamie arched her brow. "You're installing Muffin in the dashboard of *my* truck?"

"Yeah. We can't use my car. Oh, and you're going to need directions to Rawlins's place."

She looked up. "Why don't I just follow you?"

"What makes you think I'm going out there?"

"Like I said, I know you. You're dressed in your Bennett Electric uniform. Are they having electrical problems this morning by chance?"

He grinned. "As a matter of fact, they are. But you won't arrive until much later." He reached for a pen and paper and began writing directions. "You'll need a key for the cabin in case you get back before I do." He reached into his pocket and placed one on the table.

Jamie had finished her donut and was staring at the remaining ones. "Is that what I think it is?" She pointed to one.

"Yep. Chocolate-covered malted cream."

"Oh, man." She stared.

Max laughed softly. "Well, are you going to eat it or what?"

"This is between me and the donut, OK? It has nothing to do with you."

TALL WROUGHT-IRON GATES CIRCLED HARLAN Rawlins's property. The main entrance boasted a guardhouse where a uniformed man met Jamie, eyeing her truck and dog skeptically.

"Does the dog bite?" he asked.

"No, that would take effort on his part," Jamie replied.

The guard almost smiled.

"I have an appointment with Reverend Rawlins."

He checked the small notebook in his hand. "You must be Jane. The reverend is expecting you." He eyed the animal in the back. "You'll need to tie the dog out front."

"He's not as dangerous as he looks," Jamie said, "and it takes an act of God to get him out of this truck. Try going to a pet store for a dog and having to buy a truck as well."

The guard hesitated. "I suppose he looks harmless enough. Just make sure he stays in the truck." He pressed a button, and the gate swung open.

Jamie followed a cobblestone road that was flanked by pines, tupelo, firs, and red maple, interspersed with dogwood, mountain laurel, and rhododendron, the latter of which had already lost their blooms. She rounded a copse of tall loblolly pines and caught her breath at the sight of Rawlins's bricked English manor house, surrounded by parklike grounds and stone courtyards.

Jamie spied a truck with the name Bennett Electric on it. No surprise there, Max Holt was on the job, just as she'd suspected. She was relieved, but she would be slow to admit it to him.

She parked, climbed from the truck, and stood before Fleas. "How do I look? Do I have the word *easy* written all over me or what?"

The dog cocked his head to the side.

"Now hear this," Jamie said, trying to sound stern. "You so much as think about following me like you did at the motel and you're not getting any more table scraps, got it?" The dog actually seemed to sigh as he slid to the floor of the truck and propped his head on his paws. Jamie stroked one floppy ear and made kissy sounds before turning toward the house.

A brick portico sheltered the front doorway. The man who met her wore dark slacks, a crisp white shirt, and a burgundy tie. He was not smiling.

"I'm Ward Reed," he said, giving her a cursory glance, followed by a look of outright disapproval. "Reverend Rawlins is waiting for you." He opened the door wide to admit her.

Jamie stepped inside a large foyer of inlaid marble and ornate columns. She followed Reed down a long hall where he paused before a door and knocked. A voice on the other side admitted them.

"Hello, Jane," Harlan said, greeting her warmly. He took her hand in his, holding it longer than was necessary. "It's good to see you again. You can leave us now," he told Reed.

The man nodded and closed the door behind them. Jamie studied Harlan's office. It was large and paneled in teak. A triple window overlooked more gardens, a valley below, and in the distance purple mountain ranges. Rawlins's desk was tucked into one corner of the room. A stone fireplace with floor-to-ceiling bookshelves on either side—mostly religious material—took up one wall. The opposite end was decorated in earth tones, with plump sofas and chairs and a multi-print rug that seemed to pull everything together.

"Very nice," she said, trying to commit it to memory. She would describe it later in her notebook.

"I spend a lot of time in here, so it was designed for comfort." Harlan smiled. "I hope you didn't have any trouble finding the place."

"Not at all." Jamie met his gaze. She thought he looked tired. "I appreciate your inviting me to your home on such short notice, Reverend Rawlins. I hope this isn't an inconvenience."

"Of course not. Now, why don't we try to be less formal? You call me Harlan, and I'll call you Jane. Would you like something to drink? Coffee, tea, juice?" When she shook her head, he motioned toward one of the sofas. "Please sit down." He sat beside her.

"I was surprised to find a security guard out front," Jamie said.

He nodded solemnly. "I'm not crazy about the idea, but I'm afraid it's necessary."

She gave him an innocent, wide-eyed look. "Are you in danger?"

Harlan smiled gently and patted her hand. "There are people in this world who don't appreciate my spreading the Good Word. But don't worry; you're safe. Now, let's talk about you."

Jamie shrugged. "There's not much to tell. My husband and I just moved here and we were hoping to find a good church."

"You're married?"

"Just barely," she said. "My marriage is sort of on the skids right now because of my, um, indiscretions."

"Tell me a little bit about your problem, Jane. If you don't mind talking about it, that is."

"I trust you, Reverend Rawlins," she said. "I knew the minute I looked into your eyes and touched your hand last night that I could tell you anything."

"I'm glad you feel that way, dear."

Jamie sighed. "I don't know where to begin. I've just been wild as long as I can remember."

"Explain what you mean by *wild*."

"You know, loose as a goose."

"Would you say that you're promiscuous?"

"Oh, yeah." Jamie put her hand on his knee. "I can't seem to help myself."

Harlan glanced down at her hand. "Do you and your husband presently have, um, relations?"

"No. Which makes my condition worse. I'm like a walking time bomb, Harlan."

He sucked in his breath and glanced toward the closed door. "Jane, I am terribly concerned about your condition, but you must realize the danger you place yourself in each time—"

"I use protection," she interrupted.

Harlan shifted on the sofa. "Do you ever feel guilty afterward?"

"Sometimes. It doesn't stop me, though."

"Have any of these men ever hurt you?"

Jamie lifted her eyes to his. "Only when I ask them to."

• • •

"Holy crap!" Max said, listening to every word Jamie said. "What does she think she's doing?"

Lying next to Max in the crawlspace beneath Harlan Rawlins's house, Dave was busy shining his light in the dirt. "Sounds like she wants Harlan to slap her around. Some women are into that sort of thing. Can we go now?"

Max shot him a dark look. "Jamie's not like that. And we can't leave. You haven't even linked up the cameras."

"I can't believe you dragged me into this," Dave said. "This is a breeding ground for spiders and cockroaches. We're probably lying in cockroach feces at this very moment. Damn, my left eye is twitching."

Max glanced at him. "What does that mean?"

"Means I don't like it down here, that's what it means."

"Well, the sooner we get the job done, the better."

"I'm working as fast as I can."

"And you're doing a hell of a job," Max said. "You want something done right, you hire the best. That's you, Dave."

"You couldn't afford to pay me to do this," Dave grumbled. "I'm doing it out of friendship and nothing more. Hell, man, we wouldn't even know it if a spider bit us." He paused in his work. "Is it me or does the house seem to be getting lower? I feel like everything is closing in on me. I'm having trouble breathing."

"Trust me, Dave, it's you."

"Excuse me, what are the two of you doing down there?"

Max paused and glanced sideways. Ward Reed was peering beneath the house. "Man, you've got some serious problems down here," Max told him.

Reed frowned. "What kinds of problems?"

"The wires have been chewed in various places," Max said. "Looks like a raccoon did it."

"That's ridiculous."

"That's what I thought, but there's a dead raccoon down here, and he looks like he's been fried."

"Come out from beneath the house and talk to me. And bring the raccoon."

Max and Dave exchanged looks. "I don't think that's a good idea," Max said. "He looks nasty."

"I want to see him. Now."

Max crawled out from beneath the house, dragging a plastic bag with him. Inside was a dead raccoon. He dumped it at Reed's feet. "It's yours if you want it, although I don't recommend hanging it over your fireplace mantel."

"That's the most disgusting thing I've ever seen."

"I agree," Dave said, shuddering. He stepped back, eye twitching furiously.

Reed looked from Dave to Max. "What the hell is his problem?"

"He'll be OK," Max told Reed. "Just a small case of claustrophobia."

Reed sighed.

"I think maybe the raccoon was rabid and looking for water," Max said. "I noticed the pond has been drained. That would have been the first place he would have checked."

Reed shrugged. "There was a lot of algae in it, so we emptied it two days ago."

"This is the way I figure it," Max said. "We've had no rain to speak of; the creeks and rivers are drying up. If this raccoon was rabid and couldn't find water, he probably decided to look beneath the house where it's cooler. You know how crazy they get. No telling what kind of damage he did under here." He paused. "Have you ever seen a rabid coon?"

Dave gave Max his undivided attention.

Reed shook his head. "Fortunately, no."

"I'm surprised nobody noticed it," Max said, pointing to the animal. "I saw a tricycle out back, so I assume there's a child on the premises. This coon could have attacked the kid. Or worse."

Reed automatically stiffened. "Get rid of it. Nobody else is to know about this, do you understand? I don't want to hear another word about rabid raccoons on this property."

Max nodded.

"I don't care what you have to do to repair the electrical system—"

"We'll have to run new lines inside the house," Max said. "Might take a while, but Dave here is an expert."

Reed closed his eyes as if he was trying to muster up a little patience. "You'll have my full cooperation. Just get the job done as quickly and quietly as possible, and you might find a nice bonus in your check." He walked away.

Dave waited until they were alone. "Why the hell didn't you tell me you thought the coon was rabid?" he demanded.

"I was trying to make Reed believe it. The coon died because somebody ran over him.

You were there when we pulled him out of the road."

"Oh, Jesus."

"What?"

"You don't know the coon wasn't sick. And I'm pretty sure he scratched me when I was trying to help you get him into that bag." He held out his arm and pointed to a faint red line.

"There's no puncture wound, Dave. You probably scratched yourself crawling under the house."

Dave grimaced. "On a rusty nail, no doubt. Let's see, which would be worse, dying of tetanus, a fatal infectious disease marked by rigidity and spasms, or having my central nervous system attacked by rabies and suffering a horrifying drooling death?"

"You're going off on me, Dave. Noting the coon's flat-as-a-fritter body, I'm willing to take an oath that he was run over by a heavy piece of equipment, namely an automobile or truck. I mean, what does it take to convince you, man, tread marks?"

"You can make light of this all you like, but there is no cure for rabies. Once a—" He swallowed. "Once victims have been exposed they only have about seventy-two hours to be vaccinated so they can develop an immunity."

"What are the symptoms?"

"Headache and fever. Feels like the flu. It gets much worse after that, then you die."

"I'll make a deal with you. We'll watch the scratch carefully over the next few hours. If we see a change in it I'll personally take you to the ER. Now, we have work to do."

"I'm not climbing back into that hellhole," Dave said, backing away. "I'll give you instructions from out here, but I'm not going under that house."

"OK, fine, but you're going to have to calm down or you'll blow our cover." Max crawled beneath the house once more. He grabbed his headset and listened. "Dammit to hell!" he said.

Dave got on his knees. "What is it? Did something bite you?"

Max, tuned in to what was happening between Rawlins and Jamie, jerked off the headset. "Jamie just kissed Rawlins."

NICK SANTONI PUT HIS CAR INTO NEUTRAL and let the engine idle. He had followed the pickup truck from Harlan's home, keeping himself at a safe distance. He'd followed the truck to Wal-Mart and waited while the woman had gone inside, and he'd followed her to a strip of dirt road where *No Trespassing* signs dared him to come any closer.

He pulled out a pair of binoculars and watched the truck turn into a driveway, watched the woman yank off a red wig and scratch her head furiously before finger-combing her shoulder-length blonde hair into place. He smiled, picked up the photo on his seat, gave it a cursory glance.

"Welcome to Sweet Pea, Tennessee, Miss Swift," he said, and drove on.

NINE

HOLDING HER PURSE IN ONE HAND AND THE red wig in the other, Jamie climbed from her truck. Max and several men stood just outside the garage. Max introduced them. "These gentlemen are here to install Muffin inside the dashboard of the truck."

"What does Muffin have to say about all this?"

"She's raising almighty hell. Threatening to destroy her own hard drive." He paused. "So, if you won't be needing the truck for a while—"

Jamie noticed she had the men's full attention. Actually, they were gawking. She stared back. They quickly turned away as though embarrassed to have been caught staring. She tossed the keys to Max. "Go ahead. Just make sure Muffin doesn't think it was my idea." She headed for the house.

Max didn't take his eyes off her as he handed one of his engineers the keys. "Go at it, gentlemen."

"Yes, Mr. Holt," one of them said.

Max stepped inside the cabin a moment later and found Jamie's bedroom door closed. He tapped on it and walked in. He arched one brow when he found her stripping off her tank top. She quickly pulled it back on, but not before he saw the peach-colored bra. For a moment they simply stood there, staring at each other.

Jamie planted her hands on her hips. "What happened to waiting until you're invited before entering? You're lucky I don't clobber you."

He crossed his arms and leaned against the door frame. "Most women threaten to clobber me if I try to *leave* their bedroom."

Jamie did an eye roll.

Max closed the distance between them, raised a finger, and touched the strap to her tank top. When Jamie shivered, he looked up.

"OK," she said. "I give up. What do you want?"

He cocked his head to the side and smiled lazily.

"When pigs fly," she said. Still, that slow smile made her think of afternoons stretched beneath smooth sheets, legs entwined. Oh God, she was doing it again.

Max slid his fingers back and forth beneath the strap of her top. "I hope this doesn't have anything to do with Rawlins."

She blinked. "Excuse me?"

"Well, you *did* kiss him."

She snapped her head up. "How do you know about that?"

"Dave and I heard the whole thing. Unfortunately, by the time we hooked into the cameras you were gone, so we didn't actually get to see anything juicy."

Jamie felt her face burn. "You listened to our conversation?"

"Why do you think we were there? Dave and I tapped into both the phone lines and the surveillance cameras."

"I thought you were there for backup."

"How would we know you were in trouble if we couldn't hear what was going on? Or were you just planning to scream if something happened? And how else do you expect us to find out who Harlan's mob pals are if we can't hear or see the activity over there?"

Jamie knew all that in theory, of course, only she didn't like having her conversation with Harlan taped. "Well, I hope you and Dave enjoyed yourselves."

"Actually, I thought you played him pretty well."

"You did?"

"Until you kissed him."

"Oh, for Pete's sake!"

"He must have enjoyed it. He invited you to lunch tomorrow."

Jamie sighed. "That should please you. The whole point of my being here is to try to spend time with him and get information."

"Not if it puts you in danger. We already know what the man is capable of."

And then he kissed her, soft and lingering. He slipped his arms around her waist and pulled her closer.

"We're good together, Jamie. We could be better." He reached for the hem of her top and pulled it upward and over her head, exposing her bra. He kissed the valley between her breasts before unhooking the back of her bra and pulling it away.

Jamie simply stood there, not knowing what else to do, enjoying the feel of her body responding to Max. "Max? This is scary."

"Scary?"

"Complicated."

"You make it complicated."

"It's a girl thing."

"I like girl things."

She chuckled. "You're terrible."

"Can't you for once just let go and enjoy your life without knowing precisely what's going to happen next? You're willing to take all sorts of risks with Harlan Rawlins just to get your story."

"That's different."

"The things you put me through." He reached into his pocket and pulled out a miniature cell phone. He handed it to her. "My number is voice-activated. You'll be able to reach me at all times, just by calling my name. Not only will I get your call, I'll know your location. Keep it with you and turned on at all times." He started for the door, then turned. "OK?"

She nodded.

"SOMEBODY WANT TO TELL ME WHAT'S GOING on?" Muffin demanded early the next morning as Max and Jamie sat inside Jamie's pickup truck. The engineers had worked through the night, installing Muffin and welding the glove compartment shut so that nobody would be able to detect the system. Max was doing a final check before Jamie took off on her shopping trip.

"I've already explained why this was necessary," Max said. "Jamie and I have to blend in the community. I can't very well drive my car, but I'm still going to need your assistance."

"I've lost most of my capabilities," Muffin said.

"You're still hooked up to the motherboard. You'll be able to get the information I need."

"I don't have my sensors *or* my siren. I was attached to that siren."

In the back of the truck, Fleas howled.

"What was *that?*" Muffin asked.

"My dog," Jamie said. "He's a bloodhound, and his name is Fleas."

Muffin gave a snort of disgust. "I should have known something like this would happen. I'm riding in a rust bucket with a hound dog named Fleas."

"It gets worse, Muffin," Max said. "Jamie let Harlan Rawlins kiss her yesterday."

"Oh God. See what happens when you shut

me down?" Muffin accused. "I can't turn my back for one minute without you two getting into something."

"It's not what you think," Jamie said. "I was just doing my job."

"I can't believe you let him kiss you," Muffin said as though shocked and dismayed. "Is he a good kisser?"

Jamie shrugged. "Passable."

Max shook his head as he climbed from the truck and slammed the door. He turned and peered in the open window. "Look, Anderson is going to be here in a couple of hours. The three of us need to talk."

"I'll be back by then." Jamie slid beneath the wheel.

"Where on earth are you going to shop for clothes at this hour?"

"Wal-Mart."

"It's not even six A.M."

"They're open twenty-four hours a day."

"Except on Sunday," Muffin said.

Max glanced at the dashboard. "I can't believe you actually know when Wal-Mart is open." He turned to Jamie. "What could you possibly need at this hour?"

Jamie tossed him a saucy smile. "Shorter

skirts, Holt." She pulled from the driveway, leaving a frowning Max behind.

JAMIE DECIDED SHOPPING AT WAL-MART AT six in the morning had its advantages. For one thing, she had the best pick of parking spots. She promised Muffin she would hurry before climbing from the truck, and gave Fleas a firm warning to stay put. She headed for the glass doors leading inside the store.

At first Jamie didn't notice him. She was too busy thumbing through the women's department where skirts in animal prints had been marked half-price. She felt someone watching her and turned. A tall, well-dressed man with black hair was staring.

As if realizing he'd suddenly been caught, he jumped. "I'm sorry, I didn't mean to—"

She noted the desolate look in his eyes. "Are you OK?"

"Yes, well . . ." He paused and gave a pained smile. "Actually, no."

"Are you ill? Should I ask one of the employees to help you?"

"That would probably be best. If you don't mind," he added in a strained voice.

Jamie nodded and hurried off to find some-one working in women's wear.

A stout woman with short gray hair joined the man a moment later. "May I help you, sir?"

"Yes, thank you. I need to buy a dress for my sister."

Jamie continued thumbing through the clothes on a rack not far away. She was only vaguely aware of the two talking.

"What kind of dress?" the woman asked.

"Something pretty."

"What's the occasion, hon?"

The man didn't answer right away. Jamie paused in what she was doing and waited for his answer.

"Something nice enough for church," he finally said. "Do you have anything in pink? That was her favorite color." He whispered the rest.

Jamie strained to hear.

"Oh, I'm so sorry, sir," the saleslady said quietly. "Of course I'll help you. I'll need her size."

"I think she wore about a size ten. She has pretty clothes at home, but I couldn't bring my-self to go there and look through her closet. Under the circumstances," he added. "I don't like what the people at the funeral home chose for her."

Jamie moved away. From what she'd managed to hear, the man had obviously just lost his sister, and she didn't feel right listening to such a private and painful conversation. Once she'd made her purchase, she hurried into the small restaurant area, where she purchased a sprinkled donut and a cup of coffee. She took a seat at one of the tables. She'd only taken one sip of her coffee when the man she'd spotted earlier walked in, ordered coffee, and sat in a booth a short distance away.

Jamie tried not to stare, but she couldn't help it. Grief etched his face, making him look older than he probably was. He raised his coffee to his mouth, and she could see that his hands trembled badly. All at once, the cup slipped from his fingers and fell to the floor. He jumped, obviously startled.

Jamie bolted to her feet and hurried over. "Are you OK? Were you burned?"

He was already on the floor trying to mop up the mess with his napkin. He looked up as though surprised to see her. "No, I'm fine, but I made a big mess."

Jamie hurried to a counter and plucked napkins from a dispenser. She cleaned up the spill as best as she could. "You're sure you're not burned?"

"I wasn't burned, really. Thanks for helping me." He looked embarrassed. "I used to spill my milk at the dinner table, too." He tried to smile.

"Let me get you another cup of coffee," Jamie said, grabbing his cup and walking away before he had a chance to respond. She carried his cup to the cashier, who refilled it.

When Jamie returned, he was still standing. She set the cup on the table instead of handing it to him. "I'm sorry I put you to so much trouble," he said. "I promise to be more careful." He started to sit down. "Would you like to join me?"

"Well, I—"

"Maybe you'd be safer where you were." Once again, he smiled.

She noted the smile didn't reach his eyes. He looked bereft. "Hold on, I'll grab my cup and donut."

Jamie returned and slid into the seat across from him. He seemed to take great caution in raising his cup to his lips, but she noted his hands were still shaking. She met his gaze over his cup. He was dark and attractive, with a thin scar running down one side of his face that didn't detract from his looks. She wondered if he'd been in a car accident at one time.

They were silent for a moment. "I wasn't trying to eavesdrop, but I couldn't help over-hearing what you said to the saleslady," Jamie said at last. OK, so it wasn't the honest-to-goodness truth, but she didn't want to admit to being nosy. "I sort of know what you're going through," she said. "I'm sorry for your loss."

"You lost someone recently?" he asked.

"I lost my father several years ago, but sometimes it seems like yesterday."

He nodded but didn't speak.

"Would you like to talk about your sister? I'm a good listener." When he hesitated, she hurried on. "Or maybe you don't feel like it. I don't mean to pry."

"You seem like a nice person."

Jamie took a sip of her coffee and tried to think of something to say, anything that might offer comfort. She didn't want to say the wrong thing as so many people had done when she'd first suffered her loss, people who tried to make her feel better by telling her that her father was in a better place or that at least he no longer had to suffer. If only they had talked less and listened more.

"Her name was Bethany. She was my twin."

"That makes it worse, doesn't it? Her being your twin and all, that is."

"Yes. We were inseparable."

"Do you have other family?"

He shook his head. "My parents are deceased. I have a few cousins, but we haven't kept in touch."

"What you need right now is a lot of support. That's what pulled me through."

"Oh, I have plenty of friends, but I don't want to burden them." He glanced at the bag beside him. "Would you mind taking a look at the dress I chose for my sister and telling me if you think it looks OK? I had to trust the saleslady, because I don't know what to buy for this sort of thing."

"I'll be glad to look at it," Jamie said. He handed her the bag, and Jamie pulled the dress out. It was a simple pink shift.

"I probably should have gone to the mall in Knoxville and picked out something nicer, but Bethany wasn't the dressy type. She preferred simple things."

"This dress is perfect, Mr. . . ."

"Michael. Michael Juliano."

"Jane Trotter," she said, deciding it was best to use the name as long as she was in Sweet

Pea, even if she wasn't in disguise at the moment.

They shook hands. "I could use another cup of coffee," Jamie said. "How about you?"

"I'm fine, but I'll get you a cup."

Jamie was already on her feet. "I can do it." When she returned she found him talking on a cell phone. He looked angry.

"Tell the guy to come back when I'm around. He's not going to like the answer I give him, so if you or the others are afraid to stay let me know."

Jamie noted the tension in his face had brought back the deep lines around his eyes and mouth. Whatever it was, it had to be bad.

"I don't care what he says. I'm not afraid to go to the police. Look, I can't talk right now, OK?" He hung up and picked up his coffee.

"Is something wrong, Mr. Juliano?"

"Nothing I can't handle. And call me Michael." He glanced at his cell. "I just didn't need that call right now."

"You mentioned the police. Are you in some kind of danger?"

"Depends on what I'm willing to pay." He covered his eyes. "Oh, hell, I'm sorry. I shouldn't have said that."

"I don't know what this is about, but if you're being threatened—"

"I don't know if the police can help," he interrupted. "I really shouldn't be talking about this." He sighed. "I should close shop and get out," he muttered to himself, and then gave a grunt of disgust. "I thought this sort of thing only happened in Jersey or Vegas." He looked at her. "Are you from here?"

She shook her head.

"Then you probably don't know how corrupt this town is. Like a bunch of piranhas just waiting to snatch up as much money as they can from honest, hard-working people."

"Are you being blackmailed?" she whispered.

Michael glanced around the room. "I shouldn't talk about it. The last thing I want to do is drag another person into it."

"I'm a good listener, Michael, and I know how to keep my mouth shut. Especially if it might jeopardize your safety," she added.

He met her gaze. Still, he refused to talk.

Jamie realized she was pushing, and that's the last thing she wanted to do. Vera had always accused her of being too softhearted where people were concerned. Vera always said, "If there's a bleeding heart out there, you can bet Jamie is going to find it."

"I'm butting in," Jamie said. "I'm sorry. I'll leave you with your coffee." She made to get up.

"You have to swear not to repeat this."

"Yes, of course."

"You can't say anything to anyone. I mean it. I just need to talk to someone. Someone who isn't involved," he added. He smiled. "I mean, what are the chances of us running into each other again?"

She nodded.

"Someone is trying to extort money from me. It's really hard for me to deal with it at the moment after what has happened with my sister. Too many nights sitting in a hospital, eating junk food, living on caffeine. It gets to a person after a while. Thing is, I think this person is counting on my recent loss to get the upper hand."

"Who is threatening you?"

"A couple of thugs," he said. "They're acting on somebody else's behalf, of course. The man in charge probably won't show his face until it's absolutely necessary. I don't know, but I assume that's the way it works."

"Do you know this person's name? The one in charge?"

"I have an idea who he is. He has quite an operation going."

"But do you know his name?" she repeated. He frowned. She was being pushy again, and she feared it would draw his suspicion. "I mean, in case you have to go to the police," she added quickly.

He glanced down at his coffee cup. "I've already said more than I should. "The less you know, the less anyone knows, the better."

Jamie suspected she was on to something. The gods must be with her, because the last thing she had expected was to meet up with somebody who might be able to give her some information, albeit unintentionally, but answers nevertheless. She didn't have enough to go on, and she might never see the man again, which meant she had to act fast.

"Listen, Michael, I haven't eaten, either." Which was true. Her donut was untouched, and it had suddenly lost its appeal. "There must be a restaurant nearby where you can enjoy a healthy breakfast. And you really look like you need a friend."

"You don't even know me."

"I believe things happen for a reason."

"What do you mean?"

"Well . . ." She paused. She was grasping at straws. "A lot of wonderful people helped me during my time of loss. If I can say one thing to help you, I've managed to return the favor." It sounded lame in her own ears, but he suddenly nodded as if it made complete sense to him. It didn't feel right that she was lying to him, using him, to get information, but it was necessary.

"There's a little place not far from here," he said after a moment. "I go there a lot. Or I did until recently," he added.

She offered him a bright smile, hoping she could bring one to his face as well, even under his current circumstances. "Tell you what, I've got an old truck outside, but it will probably get me to the restaurant. Why don't I follow you?"

WHEN JAMIE PULLED INTO THE DRIVEWAY BEside the cabin, she found Max pacing the yard. Lord, she hadn't realized how late she was. She and Michael had talked almost two hours before she'd thought to check her watch, before she'd finally mumbled a hurried good-bye. Unfortunately, Michael had not divulged more information about those threatening to extort money from him, as though he feared he'd already said too much. That didn't mean she was giving up.

Max yanked the door open as soon as she'd parked. "Where the hell have you been?"

"I told you I was going to Wal-Mart."

"We just got back from there. You weren't in the store or the restaurant area. Your truck wasn't in the parking lot. I tried to call you a dozen times. What happened?"

"Jeez, you were spying on me?" Jamie realized she had her head cocked to the side like Fleas did when she asked him if he had to take a leak.

"No, I wasn't spying on you; I was afraid you'd broken down in the truck or that something had happened. Jesus, Jamie, you've been gone for three hours."

She saw the deep concern on his face. She wanted to tell him the truth, about Michael and their meeting, but she needed time to think about it herself. She had sworn not to utter a word of what Michael had said to her. *Sworn* to him. And rule number one for journalists was never to compromise your source. Especially when there was more information to be had. Better to keep her mouth shut. For now.

Still, not confiding everything to Max felt like lying.

"Jamie?"

"Yeah?" This time Max had his head cocked to the side.

"I lost track of the time, OK? And I must've forgotten to turn on my cell phone. I'm sorry I worried you."

Jamie saw Dave leaning against the Bennett Electric truck. He wore a thick bandage on his arm. He was staring at Fleas.

"Is that your dog?" he asked. When Jamie nodded, he gave a deep frown. "I'm allergic to dog dander. Dust mites thrive on animal dander."

"Dust mites thrive on everything, Dave," Max said, "including your own skin."

"I'm not as allergic to poodles or Italian greyhounds," Dave went on as though he hadn't heard Max. "Oh, and whippets and Mexican hairless dogs are pretty much hypoallergenic. I wish you had a poodle," he told Jamie.

Jamie looked at Fleas, who had followed her out of the truck. She tried to imagine him as a poodle and couldn't. "He's really a good dog," she said.

"Don't you take allergy shots and medication?" Max asked Dave.

Dave ignored him. "My eyes are already itching." He stepped closer to Max. "Are they red and puffy?"

"They look perfectly normal to me."

"I'll try to keep the dog away from you," Jamie promised.

Dave sighed. "I suppose I can double up on my medication. I may have to run back to the hospital for an allergy shot."

Max turned to Jamie. "Dave is going to follow us to Knoxville for your rendezvous with Rawlins."

"Us?"

"I'll drive you part of the way so I can get updates from Muffin. Once we're at the hotel, Dave and I will be close by in case something happens."

"What if Harlan recognizes you?"

"He won't see me." He paused. "Trust me, Rawlins has something up his sleeve or he wouldn't have invited you to lunch at a hotel in Knoxville."

"He's a womanizer, Max. That doesn't make him dangerous."

"What are you going to do when he suggests getting a room?"

Jamie had already considered it. And planned for it. She had purchased an extra-strength fast-acting laxative in the pharmacy at Wal-Mart, and she planned to put it in Rawlins's tea or coffee if the opportunity presented itself. It was probably the dumbest idea she'd ever had, which was why she had no intention of telling Max, but it might prove a deterrent if things got out of hand.

"I'm going to have to play it by ear, Max," she said after a moment. "I have to appear interested and hope I gain his trust without, well, you know—"

"Yeah, I know. Which brings me to the next subject," he said. "I think you should wear a wire. In case something happens."

Jamie looked from Max to Dave, then back at Max. "That's kinda risky, isn't it?"

"Going in without a wire would be more of a risk," Max replied. "Dave and I have had Rawlins under surveillance since yesterday. From what we've been able to learn through his conversations with his bodyguard, he mouthed off at the guy who's been bleeding him for money the past few years. Have you heard of the Santoni family?"

Jamie nodded. "Who hasn't? Two of them went to trial a few years back for murder."

"They whacked a cop who was on the family's payroll," Dave said. "Supposedly, it was an honest mistake, but you don't kill cops, especially the ones covering your ass."

"They got off, if I remember correctly," she said.

"The star witness literally disappeared off the face of the earth," he said, "despite around-the-clock police protection. One of the shooters, Nick Santoni, was involved in the cop killing. His uncle sent him to Tennessee, as sort of a punishment. The other shooter accidentally drowned in his bathtub."

Jamie arched one brow. "How come Nick Santoni didn't suffer the same consequences?"

"His father headed up the family until he died of a heart attack five years ago," Max said. "Nick was supposed to take his place, but the family vetoed it, and Nick's uncle was forced to come out of retirement and take over. He wanted to see Nick eventually head up the family, but it isn't likely."

"Why not?" Jamie asked.

"Nick has a habit of disobeying orders, moving in on other people's territory, you name it. He's got a chip on his shoulder and doesn't get along with the family, except for this uncle."

Jamie pondered it. "That's odd, since the uncle is the one who took what Nick would consider his rightful place."

"This uncle protects Nick," Dave said. "Not only is he Nick's godfather, Nick was always his favorite. So he sent him here, and Nick has opened shop, so to speak. He's got Rawlins by the short hairs. On top of that, we think Nick is supplying Rawlins with uppers and downers."

"The rest of the family merely tolerate Nick," Max told her, "but it looks like Nick regained their favor when he got his hooks into Rawlins. But Nick has a serious gambling problem and squanders money. Both the Santoni family and Harlan put up the money to buy my TV network but lost the bid. Harlan is convinced Nick blew the money in Atlantic City, at least that's what we heard him tell Reed, and it's a real possibility, since Nick visits the area a couple of times a month.

"Now, Nick has raised Rawlins's percentage, probably hoping to pacify the family until he can get his hands on enough money to pay them back. But Rawlins has had enough, despite the fact Nick is feeding what looks like a drug addiction. Rawlins is thinking of going over Nick's head and telling the uncle the truth."

"The mob has their own code of ethics," Dave said. "Family honor and all that. Nick is a rogue player who doesn't care who he hurts as long as he gets what he wants. And right now he wants and *needs* money. If he catches wind that Rawlins is thinking of blowing the whistle on him, he could get really dangerous."

"Either way, Nick loses," Max said. "If he has Rawlins killed or pushes him too far, there goes his meal ticket, and the family is going to wash their hands of him. If he lets Rawlins live, there's a chance he's going to be found out."

"And that could be equally bad," Dave said.

"Would Nick's own family kill him?" Jamie asked.

"It's been known to happen," Dave said. "Nick Santoni is a desperate man right now. He'll probably try to make some quick business deals in order to get his hands on money. Max and I don't know exactly what he's involved in, although it's almost a sure thing he's involved in prostitution, backroom gambling, drugs, and probably gunrunning, just to name a few. We tapped into his computer yesterday, but we haven't been able to decipher the information."

"It's all coded," Max said. "The codes are

similar to those used by the CIA, but damned if I've been able to crack them. We need more time."

"That's why we're concerned about your meeting with Rawlins," Dave said. "Harlan's bodyguard checks for bugs in the office and home every day, but Nick may have found a way to prevent detection. We did it by hooking into the phones and cameras."

"What it boils down to," Max said, "is we don't know what Nick knows. If he even suspects Harlan might go over his head there's going to be trouble. Big trouble. And you just might find yourself right in the middle of it."

TEN

"WHY DIDN'T YOU TELL ME THIS SOONER?"
Jamie asked.

"We're gathering information as we speak,"
Max said. "While you've been, um, shopping,
Muffin has been hard at work tapping into
every resource she can find. She's been
e-mailing information to us as she gets it." He
paused. "I'm not holding back anything, if
that's what you think."

Which explained why Muffin hadn't questioned Jamie when she had returned to the
truck after having breakfast with Michael, she
thought. Muffin had been preoccupied. And Jamie hadn't offered an explanation because she
knew Muffin would say something to Max.

And then Max would interrogate her to the nth degree about Michael.

Jamie was determined to get information from Michael, which was why she had suggested they meet again the following day. But she was going to be careful and subtle about it. Max had his mighty computer and enough contacts to overthrow a small country, but she had genuine empathy for people, and she hoped Michael would sense it and open up. She felt a little guilty about using him when he was grieving and probably at his most vulnerable, but she might be able to help him in the end as well. If she did learn something, if it was something that could put Michael in danger, then she would have reason enough to break her oath and tell Max.

She suddenly realized Max was talking to her.

". . . So far we don't have much on Santoni. Other than a couple of photos of him ducking in and out of the courtroom during his trial," he added. "They're not very clear. Also, he wore a beard at the time, so he could look completely different today. He has a number of aliases, which make it hard to get an address or anything else on him.

"I suspect he stays in the background as

much as possible. He's probably got a couple of men he trusts who see that his orders are followed. Which is how it usually works for those in the upper echelon; they look like legitimate businessmen, but the businesses are merely fronts for illegal activity."

"Do you think Nick Santoni hired Vito Puccini and ordered the hit on you?"

Max nodded. "We have it on tape. Harlan discussed it with his bodyguard at length after Santoni paid him a visit yesterday. Rawlins had nothing to do with arranging it, but I think he suspected something was going on, and for some reason he decided not to go to the police. Which leads me to believe Santoni has something on him," he added. "Rawlins might be a lot of things, but he's probably not a killer. We still think you should wear a wire. In case there are any surprises."

Jamie didn't look convinced.

"It's like this," Max said. "I don't like the idea of your meeting with Harlan in the first place, but it's already set up, so I'll agree to it, but *only* if you're wired. I want to know where you are at all times. Otherwise, I'm calling this whole thing off."

He and Jamie locked gazes in a battle of

wills. "What if Harlan discovers the wire?" she asked.

Max met her gaze. "That's not likely to happen as long as you keep your clothes on, Swifty."

MUFFIN GREETED MAX AND JAMIE IN A SURLY voice when they climbed into the truck at ten-thirty for the drive to Knoxville. "That dog whines constantly. I don't like it."

"I know he's an inconvenience right now, Muffin," Jamie said, "but I don't know what to do with him."

"Try the animal shelter."

"Nobody would adopt him."

"Is he ugly?"

Jamie and Max both glanced over their shoulders at Fleas, who had his face pressed against the back window. Max shrugged; Jamie grinned. "Actually, he's pretty cute," she said.

"I guess it could be worse," Muffin said. "I guess I could be strapped to a moped or tied to the back of a mule."

"You should feel flattered that we need you so badly," Jamie told her as Max pulled from the driveway with Dave following. She glanced at Max. He looked distracted; Jamie knew he was worried.

"This is your big day, huh?" Muffin said. "You're having lunch with Rawlins."

"Uh-huh."

"You wearing your slut outfit?"

"No, I toned it down since we're meeting at the Hyatt Regency."

"Her skirt is a little short," Max said, "and she's wearing a push-up bra. If she sneezes she's going to pop out all over the place."

"And get this, Muffin," Jamie said. "I'm wearing a wire."

"You planning on doing the nasty?" Muffin asked.

Jamie gave a burst of laughter. "I don't believe you said that."

"Because if you are, you're going to have to excuse yourself and go to the rest room so you can remove that wire. Things get too hot, it might short-circuit on you."

"Time to change the subject," Max said. "You got anything new for me?"

"I'm still trying to find an address for Santoni. The man doesn't exist on paper, not even under the aliases he's used. Doesn't own property, doesn't even pay a light bill. I figure his family got all new identification for him when he relocated to Knoxville."

"Maybe he lives in Sweet Pea," Max said. "A man like that would enjoy the seclusion this area offers."

"I'll keep looking. As for looking into Harlan Rawlins, I've checked police records within a three-hundred-mile radius. There's a lot of domestic violence in this part of the country, which I attribute to financial stress. The unemployment rate here is very high. Harlan has never been arrested, but I did find something interesting when I checked the local hospital records. Harlan's wife has visited the emergency room twice, once for a fractured wrist which she claimed happened as a result of falling off her horse, and another time with a concussion when the same horse threw her and she hit her head against a tree."

"It sounds legit," Jamie said.

"Sounds like she needs to get rid of the horse," Max said. "Or Rawlins," he added. "If he was actually abusing his wife and Santoni knew, that in itself could be cause for blackmail." He pulled into the parking lot of a gas station. "The Hyatt is less than a mile from here. Dave and I will follow you. We'll be close by at all times.

"Now listen to me, Jamie. If Harlan suggests going upstairs to a room, I want you to get the number to me. I don't care how you do it, work it into the conversation somehow, but make sure you say it loud enough for me to hear."

Jamie nodded. "I'll be OK, Max."

"One last thing. If there are any surprises, scream like hell. Dave and I will kick in the door if we have to, but I don't want you taking chances. I don't care if we blow the case or not when it comes to your safety."

"I'll be careful, I promise."

They climbed from the truck, and Jamie got in on the driver's side. As she put it into gear, she noticed her hand was trembling. She pulled onto the street once more and headed for the hotel.

Jamie noted the strange look on the valet's face as she pulled up to the Hyatt entrance. She didn't know if he was more amazed at the amount of rust on the truck or the sight of Fleas in back.

She handed the young man her key and smiled. "It's an antique," she said, motioning to the truck. "Please see that you don't put a scratch on it."

He remained straight-faced. "Yes, ma'am. I'll take good care of it. What about the dog?"

"He'll be fine. He's got food and water back there."

"You're not worried someone might take him?"

Jamie patted her wig into place. "Would you be if you were me?"

He looked at the animal. "On second thought, no."

Ward Reed was waiting for Jamie in the lobby. He motioned her toward the elevator. "Reverend Rawlins decided to order lunch in his private suite," he said. "I hope you don't mind."

Jamie couldn't hide her surprise. She hoped Max and Dave were nearby. "The reverend actually keeps a suite here?" she said, voice raised in surprise. "Oh, my. His own suite."

"He often has business in Knoxville. He also invites guests from time to time, you know, visiting clergy? There aren't any nice hotels in Sweet Pea."

Jamie knew about the hotels in Sweet Pea.

The elevator doors opened, and they waited for the people to clear out before entering. Jamie could feel the tension in the back of her neck. Reed punched a number, and she realized they were going to the top floor. "Wow, we're going all the way to the top? I'll bet there is a great view from up there."

Reed smiled stiffly. "Yes. Reverend Rawlins says he feels closer to heaven."

Jamie nodded as though it made perfect sense. She tried to remain calm as the express elevator whooshed them upward, but the thought of going to Harlan's private suite was a little unnerving. Then she reminded herself of the great story she would have when it was over, and that spurred her confidence.

A bell rang out, interrupting her thoughts.

"Here we are," Reed announced, holding the doors so Jamie could exit first. She followed him to a door at the end of the hall. "Oh, my, would you look at that! Room Twelve-ten. That's my birthday, December tenth. But don't you dare ask the year." She laughed at her own joke. Reed merely nodded. Jamie decided he didn't have much of a sense of humor.

He tapped lightly on the door and inserted a card into the lock. He pushed the door open. "Go on in. I'll escort you down when you're ready to leave."

Inside, Jamie found a large, beautifully decorated living room with a kitchenette. Fresh flowers sat on the coffee table.

Harlan stepped through a set of sliding glass

doors that led outside onto the balcony. He smiled. "Welcome, Jane."

"Your suite is very nice," she said.

"Thank you." He walked over and touched one of her red curls, toyed with it. His gaze met hers. "I'm glad you came." His finger slid down her cheek, brushed her neck, and rested on her shoulder. "I sometimes come here to unwind or write my sermons."

Or get laid, Jamie thought. "We all need time to ourselves," she said. "I imagine it gets hectic touring all the time."

"Yes, it does." He took her hands in his. "But spending this time with you is a real treat. Would you like something to drink?" He nodded toward a basket of fruit and a bottle of wine. "I don't usually drink alcohol, but a dear friend left this for me, and I hate to waste it. I'm not particularly fond of the red wine. It tastes bitter to me. But if you like it, I'll join you."

That just might work in her favor, Jamie thought. "Yes, let's have a glass."

He grinned and uncorked the bottle. "I took the liberty of ordering lunch. I hope you like fish." He looked up and caught her staring. "Is something wrong?"

"You look tired, Harlan." Which was true.

"Why don't you go out on the balcony, prop your legs, and I'll pour the wine?"

He nodded. "Promise not to take too long?"

"I'll be right out." Jamie waited until he stepped outside before she poured the wine into two glasses. Once again, her fingers trembled as she reached into her pocket for one of the laxatives she'd crushed into a fine, white powder. She sprinkled it into his drink. She stirred it, taking care to see there was no residue on the side of the glass. She had about twenty minutes before it would start to work and then she could make her getaway.

"I know what you're doing," Harlan said the minute she joined him on the balcony.

Jamie froze. "You do?"

"You're trying to spoil me."

She relaxed. "Looks like you need spoiling. Here, drink this. Maybe you'll feel better."

He took the glass. "Do I really look that tired?"

"Oh, now I've gone and hurt your feelings."

"No, actually I appreciate your honesty. I haven't slept well lately, except for last night, but I think I just need to catch up on my rest." He took out a small pillbox, opened it, and took out several tiny pills.

Jamie noticed he was trembling. "Are you OK?" she asked.

"I have a little headache. These help." He popped them into his mouth, then raised his glass to his lips.

Jamie watched closely as he took a sip of his wine. He didn't seem to notice a difference. "Losing sleep will catch up with you sooner or later. Are you worried about something?"

He shrugged. "Just everyday stress, but I don't want to burden you with it. We're here to enjoy ourselves." He drained his glass. "Perhaps I should have another," he said.

Jamie studied him. "It's none of my business, Harlan, but I don't think you should be mixing alcohol with your medication."

He nodded. "You're probably right."

"You look very handsome today in that navy blue suit," she finally said. "That's definitely your color. I'll bet half the women in your congregation have a crush on you."

He smiled and tugged at his tie as though it was too tight. "Well, I do get my share of homemade cakes and pies."

"I'll bet you do," she said, a teasing lilt in her voice.

"There are a lot of lonely widows in the

church. They just want someone to talk to, you know? I try to do my best."

"I'm sure you do." She sighed. "I know what it's like, Harlan. Not having anyone you can tell your troubles to. We all need someone we can trust. Someone who won't judge us or betray our confidence."

"People like that are hard to find," he said.

"My friends have always been able to come to me," Jamie said softly. "What good is a friend if you can't talk to them? I mean *really* talk to them," she added. "Unload, spill your guts, get it all off your shoulders kind of talk. I've heard it all, Harlan, buh-lieve you me. Nothing would shock me."

"That kind of friendship is rare indeed," he agreed.

"And I know about loneliness," she said. "The kind of loneliness you spoke of in your sermon. Sometimes . . ." She paused, as though wrestling with her emotions.

"What is it, dear?"

"Sometimes I get so lonely my skin aches."

Harlan looked at her, studied her face. "Then you know what it's like. I've discovered I have to find solace wherever I can. *However* I can."

A knock at the door seemed to startle him. "That must be our lunch." He stood and walked inside, and Jamie followed. She wondered if it was her imagination, but he seemed to move sluggishly.

"Room service," a man announced.

Jamie thought she recognized the voice. Harlan opened the door, and Jamie felt her mouth drop open at the sight of Dave pushing in a food cart. He was dressed in a hotel uniform, and he wore a mustache and glasses. She wondered if he had counted the dust mites in the mustache before he'd put it on.

"Good afternoon," he said formally. "I believe you're expecting lunch?"

Harlan nodded. "Yes, we are."

"I'll have you set up in just a jiffy," Dave said, giving Jamie a private look. He pushed the cart to the table and began setting it, placing the utensils in their proper spots. "How are you today, ma'am?" he asked.

Jamie wondered how he had managed to get a uniform from the Hyatt. No telling what he and Max were up to. "I'm, uh, fine."

Dave set the dishes on the table and lifted a metal food warmer from the plates. Jamie eyed the food appreciatively: baked fish covered in a cream sauce, new potatoes, fresh asparagus, and a Caesar salad. Dessert consisted of pecan pie, a big favorite of hers.

Dave pulled out a chair for her. Jamie walked over to the table and allowed him to seat her.

"Will there be anything else?" Dave asked.

"That will be all," Harlan said.

Dave turned to leave. He paused at the door and gave Jamie the thumbs-up.

Jamie tasted her food. "It's delicious." Harlan was staring at his plate. "Is something wrong?"

"I'm afraid I don't have much of an appetite."

"Oh, no. At least taste the fish. It's delicious. And you need to keep up your strength."

Harlan glanced up in surprise, as if he wasn't sure what she meant by the remark. Nevertheless, he forked a small amount of the fish and took a bite. "You're right. It's very good." He smiled, as if trying to put on a brave front.

"Thank you for inviting me," Jamie said. "It's not often that I get to dine on gourmet cooking in such grand surroundings."

"I hope you're not offended that I asked you to my hotel suite."

Jamie looked down at her lap. "I wouldn't blame you if you didn't want to be seen with me in public."

"Oh, no, Jane, it's nothing like that."

"I mean, I've probably slept with half the men in this hotel."

He gasped.

"I'm teasing, Harlan. You're going to have to lighten up."

"You have a very unusual sense of humor. But I should be thanking you. It's a treat for me to share lunch with a woman who is not only beautiful but has a wonderful sense of humor." He put down his fork, mopping his brow with his napkin.

"Jane, I've been looking into your, er, addiction."

"Is there a cure?" she asked hopefully, fork paused in midair. "Or am I destined to be a sex maniac for the rest of my life?"

He looked taken aback by the remark. "Don't be ashamed of who or what you are, Jane. Your creator loves you no matter what. You know, I studied psychology in seminary because I wanted to be able to help people with their problems."

"That's why you're so easy to talk to. You're a very sensitive man when it comes to other people's needs." Jamie noticed he was perspiring heavily.

He mopped his upper lip. "I try to be. I sense

you have a lot of needs that have not been addressed."

"You're so right, Harlan."

"From what I understand most sexual addictions are the result of either physical or emotional trauma suffered in childhood. Might I ask, as your minister, if that applies to you?"

Jamie glanced away. "I can't talk about it, Harlan. Perhaps in time."

He reached across the table and covered her hand. "We have all the time in the world, Jane."

His hand was clammy. Jamie leaned closer. "I suppose I don't feel I have much to offer a man. Except my body," she whispered. "You probably wouldn't understand, what with you being a godly man."

"I'm human, Jane. Do you think I didn't feel anything when you kissed me yesterday? Do you think I don't notice how attractive you are?"

"I'm so ashamed of myself for kissing you," she said. "You must think badly of me."

"Nonsense." He studied her closely, as if trying to read her thoughts.

Jamie took a deep breath, stood, and walked over to the sliding glass doors. "I think maybe we have something special."

Harlan joined her, placing his hands on her arms, sliding them downward. Very gently he lowered his head and pressed his lips to the nape of her neck.

"Oh, Harlan!"

"Sweet Jane. I can't stand to see you hurting." He turned her around in his arms and looked into her eyes.

IN THE NEXT ROOM, MAX TORE OFF THE HEADset. "Oh, damn, it's quiet in there. She must be kissing him again. What the hell are we supposed to do *now*?"

Dave shrugged. "Jamie can take care of herself. How long do I have to wear this mustache?"

"Until we finish the job." Max grabbed his headset once more and winced when a loud squeal hit his eardrums. He yanked it off. "What was *that*?"

Dave had already removed his. "Hell if I know. Oh, great, my ears are ringing."

"Something's wrong," Max said.

"Damn right. That noise set off my tinnitus. Sounds like church bells going off in my head."

"I can't make out their words. There's a lot of static. Shit."

HARLAN SUDDENLY GAVE JAMIE A FUNNY look.

"What's wrong?" she asked.

"I don't feel so good." He gripped his stomach and swayed.

Jamie tried to steady him. He looked pale. "You need to lie down."

"I'm dizzy."

"Get on the bed, Harlan!"

MAX MANAGED TO CATCH THE LAST SENtence. "Did you hear that?" he said, trying to listen to the voices through the static. "She told him to get on the bed!"

"I can't hear a thing," Dave said. "Except for static and bells. I'll probably end up losing my hearing after this."

"You need to get back over there."

Dave shook his head. "I can't just barge in."

HARLAN STRUGGLED WITH THE KNOT ON HIS tie.

Jamie saw that he was having difficulty breathing. She began to panic. "Let me help you." She didn't know what to do. She had obviously given Harlan too much laxative and it was causing him painful stomach cramps. Or maybe he was having an adverse reaction to them.

He pulled his knees against his stomach and groaned aloud. "I can't stand it!"

Jamie's heart fluttered. He was sweating profusely; his color didn't look good. "Try to take a deep breath."

"I'm going to be sick!" he cried. "Please help me to the bathroom." He covered his mouth with his hands.

Jamie scrambled to help him, but he could barely stand. She struggled to keep him upright. Lord, she'd gone and done it now. If he was having an allergic reaction there was no telling what would happen. She managed to get him inside the bathroom. He slammed the door and locked it, and the next thing Jamie heard was a loud thud. She tried the knob. "Shit! Harlan, unlock the door."

Jamie picked up the phone to call for help but dropped it when she heard a knock on the living room door. She raced toward it. Dave stood on the other side wearing the hotel uniform. "I came for your dirty dishes, ma'am," he said.

Jamie grabbed his arm and pulled him toward the bedroom. "Something is wrong with Harlan. He's in the bathroom, and I can't get in. I think he fell."

Dave reached into his pocket and pulled out a knife. He opened it up, and Jamie saw it was equipped with all sorts of gadgets. In a few seconds he picked the lock and turned the knob.

They found Harlan sprawled on the bathroom floor. Dave shook him, but there was no response. He reached down and pressed his fingers against Harlan's neck as Jamie stood there, wringing her hands.

Finally, Dave removed his hand. He shuddered. "Oh, Jesus Christ! He's dead! I touched a dead man!"

ELEVEN

MAX AND JAMIE LEFT THE HOTEL IMMEDI-
ately. Using his cell phone, which Max assured
couldn't be traced, he called 911, and, claiming
to be a security guard for the Hyatt Regency,
reported that a man had become ill in room
1210 and was in grave condition. Max didn't
bother to mention the man was already dead.
He hung up before the dispatcher questioned
him further.

Jamie, who'd struggled to maintain her com-
posure while the valet went for her truck, fell
apart the minute Max pulled onto the street and
headed for the interstate. "Oh God, everybody
is going to think I killed him!" she cried. "The
mob is going to find out who I am and hunt
me down like a dog until they—" She paused

and made a slicing motion across her throat.

"Would you calm down!" Max said.

"And what if I did kill him? What if he had a severe reaction to the laxative I put in his drink? Oh God."

"How many did you give him?"

"Two. I crushed them into a powder and put them in his drink."

"You didn't bother to tell me that."

"I figured you would think it was silly."

"People don't die from an over-the-counter laxative," Max said. "Now, calm down until I can get us out of here." He turned onto the interstate and sped up.

"What is all this noise about?" Muffin demanded. "I'm trying to download an e-card from my laptop friend at MIT and I can't think straight for all this noise."

"Harlan Rawlins is dead," Jamie said. "I was the last one to see him alive. Somehow they're going to find out who I am, and I'll end up on *Unsolved Mysteries*." She gulped. "Vera will find out. She'll probably be the one to turn me in."

"I'm not easily confused," Muffin said, "but you're not making any sense."

Max filled her in. Finally, he exited at a rest

area and backed into a slot far away from the other motorists. He reached behind the seat and pulled out a license plate and a screwdriver.

"What are you doing?" Jamie asked.

"Covering our butts in case somebody got a look at the truck and wrote down the tag number. I always keep an extra on hand."

"Do you know how that sounds?" Jamie asked. "I can't believe I'm associating with a man who carries an extra license plate wherever he goes. That is scary."

"It works for me," he said, climbing from the truck.

Jamie leaned back against the seat and closed her eyes. All she could see was Harlan's face as he'd looked in death. "Oh God," she said.

"Calm down, Jamie," Muffin said gently.

"I'm going to prison," Jamie said dully. "They'll put me on the chain gang. I could get the death penalty. What will I do with Fleas? Nobody is going to want him. They'll put him to sleep." She turned around and glanced at the bed of the truck where Fleas was sleeping.

"You're not going to prison," Muffin said. "Max will make a few telephone calls and—"

"And clear me of a murder rap? I don't think so."

Max opened the door. "Lose the wig."

Jamie looked at him. "Excuse me?"

"Give it to me."

Jamie plucked it from her head. She watched Max toss the wig and license plate into a trash can. He returned and stashed the screwdriver behind the seat before climbing in.

"That's not going to do any good. My fingerprints are all over the hotel room."

Max shook his head. "Dave wiped everything down while I was trying to revive Harlan. He's good at that sort of thing since he hates germs."

Jamie rolled her eyes. Dave had almost gone off the deep end after touching Harlan. "You seem to forget there was a witness, Max. Harlan's bodyguard personally escorted me to the room."

"You were in disguise. And a damn good one at that," he added. "Nobody is going to recognize you once you wash off all that makeup."

"The police are going to lock me up and throw away the key."

"You're not going to prison," Max said. "I don't know what happened to Harlan, but I know you didn't have anything to do with it.

Unless he got so excited with you he had a heart attack."

"What?"

"Sounded like things got pretty hot in there. You were trying to get him undressed and into bed."

Jamie gaped at him. "Excuse me?"

"Oh, brother," Muffin said. "I don't think I want to hear this."

"I heard it all," Max said. "I was afraid something like this would happen."

"Max, I don't think this is a good time to discuss what happened between Jamie and Harlan," Muffin told him. "I think we need to be a little more sensitive to her feelings."

Jamie looked at Max and shook her head. "Relax. Nothing happened."

"What?"

"Harlan got sick. I was trying to loosen his clothing so he could breathe. If I was trying to get him to lie down it was because I thought he was going to pass out." She gave him a sidelong glance. "You seem to really want to know all the details."

"Where you're concerned? Absolutely."

"Well, forget it. We need to figure out who killed Rawlins."

WARD REED SAT QUIETLY IN THE LIVING ROOM
of Harlan's suite as the detectives examined the
man's body. The medical examiner had already
been summoned, and they were awaiting him
to pronounce Rawlins dead, despite all obvious
appearances. An officer carefully wrapped the
plates of food on the table while another dusted
the room for fingerprints.

A young detective with a neat beard stood
in the kitchen questioning the officer who'd
first responded to the call. Finally, the detective
joined Reed.

"I'm Detective Sills of the Knoxville Police
Department," he said. "You're Ward Reed?"

He nodded. "I was Harlan Rawlins's bodyguard," he said.

Detective Sills sat down. "I've read your
statement, Mr. Reed. You say you escorted a
woman to the reverend's room this afternoon?"

"That's correct. I unlocked the door and let
her in."

"And she said her name was Jane? She never
gave you a last name?"

"No."

"Reverend Rawlins was to have lunch with
her?"

"Yes."

"Was Reverend Rawlins alive when this Jane person arrived?"

"I didn't see him, but I heard him call out to her as I closed the door and put the *Do Not Disturb* sign on it."

"You also said you had seen Jane at the last church service."

Reed nodded. "And she visited the reverend in his home yesterday as well."

"Is it possible he might have listed her full name in his appointment book?"

"If he knew it, he would have, but he referred to her only as Jane when he asked me to notify the security guard at the front gate of the appointment. I can check."

"I'm sending a couple of my men over. They'll go through the reverend's things and question the guard."

"You'll give me time to break the news to Mrs. Rawlins first, right?"

"My men will have to follow you over, Mr. Reed. We'll want the reverend's office and personal belongings secured immediately." The detective made notes on his pad. "Did Reverend Rawlins often meet women here?"

"Do I have to answer that question?"

Sills shrugged. "You can answer it either here or at the station."

"Am I a suspect? Do I need an attorney?"

"This is normal procedure, Mr. Reed. Your answers will help in the investigation. As one of his most trusted employees, I'm certain you'll want this case solved as quickly as we do."

Reed sighed heavily. "Yes, he often met women here."

"Did you personally escort these women up to meet the reverend?"

"Yes."

"Can you remember their names?"

"It was really none of my business to know their names or why they were visiting, and I never felt the need to inquire. Had I thought the reverend was taking a risk, I would not have brought them up."

"You'll call me if you happen to remember any of their names?"

"Of course." He checked his wristwatch. "Is this going to take long? I really need to get back to the house and break the news to his wife."

"Be patient, Mr. Reed, I promise I won't keep you any longer than I have to. Do you think you could give an accurate description of this Jane person to our artist at the station? I'd like to have a composite drawing. After you speak to Mrs. Rawlins, of course."

Reed nodded. "I'll do my best."

The medical examiner, a heavy-set man whose double chin bulged over his shirt collar, walked into the room. "I'm done," he said.

"What can you tell me?" Sills asked.

"He's deader'n hell."

Sills sighed and muttered, "Thanks a lot."

The heavy man nodded. "I found pills on him, looks like amphetamines and barbs, but we won't know for sure until the crime lab checks them out." He shrugged. "But it doesn't take a rocket scientist to figure out what killed him. His throat was slit right through the carotid artery."

"HOLY HELL!" DAVE SAID, POINTING AT THE TV.

"What now?" Max said.

Dave sat in front of the TV, a magnifying glass in his hand. He'd been checking his wound again, despite the fact a doctor in the emergency room had assured him it didn't look like a bite and there was no need to be vaccinated for rabies.

Max followed Dave's gaze to the TV set,

where the Knoxville chief of police was holding up a composite drawing of Jamie in her disguise. Max didn't realize Jamie had followed him into the room until he heard her gasp out loud.

"Oh, my God," she said.

"It gets worse," Dave told them. "The medical examiner was just on, and you won't believe what he said." Max and Jamie looked at him. "Rawlins's throat was cut from ear to ear."

"Jesus," Max said. "He wasn't like that when we last saw him."

Jamie nodded. "Somebody came into the room after we left. Before the police arrived."

"Why would somebody slit his throat?" Max asked. "He was already dead."

Dave looked up. "Here's one even better. What if the killer had been there the whole time? Just waiting," he added. "Hell, he could have been hiding behind the shower curtain."

Jamie felt a sudden chill. "Somebody wanted to make certain he was dead. That somebody wanted to make one hundred percent certain that Harlan Rawlins never drew breath again."

"Or talked," Max added.

∙ ∙ ∙

"JAMIE, CAN I COME IN?" MAX SAID, KNOCK-
ing softly.

He heard a click, and the door opened. Jamie
stood there, her arms folded across her stomach. She wore cutoff jeans and a thin white
T-shirt.

"Are you OK?" Max asked, trying not to
stare at her breasts, but he could see her nipples
against the shirt.

Jamie shrugged and backed away from the
door. "I've been better."

Max went inside. Fleas was lying on the
floor beside her bed, having been relegated to
that part of the house because of Dave's allergies. Although the dog didn't raise his head,
his eyes followed Max as he stepped closer to
Jamie. "I feel crummy, too, Jamie. I know
Rawlins was a thief and a liar—"

"Not to mention an adulterer," Jamie added.
"He probably abused his wife as well."

"Probably."

"I feel bad about Rawlins," she said, "but
that's not why I'm freaked out. I'm scared to
close my eyes, Max. I keep thinking about
what Dave said. The murderer could very well
have been in the hotel room when Harlan and

I were there. I don't remember if the shower curtain was closed, but it would have been a perfect place to hide. What if—"

"Stop asking yourself *what if*," Max said. "The killer wasn't interested in hurting you; he wanted Harlan."

"I can't shake the feeling that he's going to get me next. Every time I close my eyes I imagine him standing over me by my bed. Watching me. I don't think I'll ever be able to close my eyes again."

Max walked over to the bed and pulled the covers aside. "Why don't you lie down, and I'll sit with you?"

Jamie lay on the bed. Max tried not to stare at her long legs.

He sat down on the edge and regarded her. "This is why I didn't want you to come with me," he said. "I was afraid something like this would happen."

"I know. But all I could think about was getting my big story. Now Harlan's dead. I don't have the story, and I wasn't able to get any information from him before he was murdered."

"You got an invitation to his private residence," Max said. "He invited you to lunch. I

think he would have told you something if he
hadn't died."

"You're just trying to make me feel better."

"No, Jamie. I believe Harlan desperately
needed someone he could talk to. I believe he
trusted you." Max reached up and pulled a
stray lock of hair from her face. "I'm glad we
got rid of that wig. Your hair is too pretty to
cover up." He let his hand rest against her
cheek for a moment.

Jamie swallowed. His touch was so tender
she felt something in her stomach flutter. "We
have to find out who killed him, Max."

"I definitely think Santoni is responsible."

"He could have hired a woman to pass herself off as a maid. That way she could have
had access to the room."

"Most women don't kill with a knife, and
from the description on the news it was very
brutal. Of course, a knife is quiet and comes
in handy when one has to worry about noise,
so that would change things. It could have been
a man dressed as a woman."

"What about Ward Reed, the bodyguard?"
Jamie asked. "He certainly had opportunity.
Maybe Santoni got to him, offered him a ton
of money."

"Or maybe Reed was already working for Santoni," Max said.

"What makes you think it wasn't Santoni himself?"

"I don't know that it wasn't, but most mob figures in his position would have hired it out because the risk would be too great. Not that Santoni isn't a risk-taker," he added. "He's taken so many risks that most of his family is against him. All I know is, whoever killed Harlan knew exactly what he was doing."

"Meaning this person has killed before and is going to kill again."

"Not necessarily. I think he got what he wanted. Let's not talk about it anymore tonight, OK? You need to try and rest." He stood.

"Max?"

"Yeah?"

Jamie was almost embarrassed to ask. "Would you sleep in here tonight?"

His look softened. "Are you sure Fleas won't mind?" he asked, as though hoping he could tease her into feeling better.

"He'll understand."

"OK." Max cut the light, rounded the bed, and kicked off his shoes.

Jamie felt the mattress dip under his weight as he lay down on the bed. He reached for her, pulled her close. Jamie lay there, her back flush against his chest. She could smell his after-shave, feel his breath on her neck. She allowed his warmth to seep in, allowed her body to relax for the first time since they'd found Harlan dead.

"Damn, Swifty, you feel good," he whispered.

"Yeah?"

"Yeah." Max adjusted his body so that she wouldn't know just how good she did feel against him.

Jamie's body responded to his nearness, the protective arm that held her close. She felt safe for the first time since finding Harlan sprawled on the bathroom floor. She shifted on the bed, trying to get closer.

"Don't do that," Max muttered, in a pained voice.

Jamie was acutely conscious of his body against hers, the hard lines that made her feel so secure. She and Max might have differences from time to time, but she knew instinctively that he would protect her no matter what. It gave her some satisfaction to know that he was as conscious of her body as she was of his. She smiled in the darkness. She was thankful she could find something to smile about after her day. "Don't do what?" she said after a moment.

"Dammit, Jamie, you know what you do to me."

"No, tell me." Even as she said it she wondered why she was teasing him. Perhaps she was simply looking for escape in Max's arms, or maybe she liked knowing Max desired her.

"I think it's obvious," Max said after a moment.

Jamie heard the smile in his voice. "Max, I know we don't always see eye-to-eye. I know you find me disagreeable at times."

"Uh-huh."

"But I appreciate your being here with me."

"Why wouldn't I? You know how I feel about you, Jamie. It's not like I haven't told you."

She took a deep shuddering breath. "I know you care about me, Max, but I think a big part is due to . . ." She paused.

"My attraction to you? Of course I'm attracted to you." He tightened his arm around her. "You make me crazy sometimes."

She heard the huskiness in his voice and something more. A need. She knew how he felt. She had tried to fight her attraction to Max from the moment she'd laid eyes on him, had tried to fight her feelings. But there was no denying it. She had never been so drawn to a man, and that's what scared her.

God, where was her self-control? she thought.

Max rose on his elbows and turned her over so that he was facing her in the dark. "Man, oh man," he whispered.

Jamie could barely make out the outline of his face, but she knew he wanted to kiss her. And, dammit, she wanted it as much as he did. It didn't seem to matter what was happening in her life; Max could just look at her a certain way or touch her and everything else faded into the background. She was obviously not a disciplined person where Max Holt was concerned.

Max found her lips. Jamie didn't hesitate to let him in; she was just as eager as he was for the kiss. He slipped his hand beneath her T-shirt, and her stomach did a massive somersault. Nope, no discipline, she thought. The man was intent on turning her on, and she was more than obliging.

Max broke the kiss, but his mouth never stilled, moving over her face in sweet lingering kisses that made her feel shivery one moment, anxious the next. She arched against him, heat seeking heat, feeling as though she couldn't get close enough. Max eased her lacy bra upward, exposing both breasts. He covered one with his mouth. Jamie closed her eyes, thinking maybe it wasn't such a bad thing to let her resolve weaken from time to time. This seemed like a good time.

His hands were warm against her cool skin. Her stomach fluttered and she could almost feel her bones turning soft and mushy.

His gentle massage sent erotic messages low in her belly. Damned if the man didn't have a way with his hands.

Max ran his hand lightly down her abdomen to her inner thighs, and Jamie knew she was a goner. Oh God, oh God, oh God. Max's hand moved higher and he turned it over so that his palm lay flat between her thighs.

Jamie sucked in her breath. She tried to think, but all logic had gone out the window. She had tried so hard to be strong. She had wanted reassurances from Max, but maybe he was right. Maybe she expected too much. There weren't any guarantees in life. Or maybe she was just rationalizing because, well, because she wanted him to make love to her.

As if sensing a subtle change in her, Max pulled back, and his hands stilled. "You're doing it again," he said. "You're thinking too much."

"I can't help it."

"Do you want me to stop?"

"Um, I don't know."

He gave an enormous sigh, pulled her T-shirt in place, and rolled onto his back.

She should never have let things go this far, she thought, only to back out in the end. What was wrong with her? What the hell was wrong with her?

"Max?"

"Go to sleep, Jamie," he said softly.

MAX WAS READING THE NEWSPAPER WHEN JAmie stumbled from the bedroom the next morning in her crumpled T-shirt. Fleas followed closely, and when Jamie stopped to open the front door, he bumped into her. Jamie turned, and they just looked at each other.

"Is there a problem?" she asked the dog.

He inched out the door as though he had all the time in the world. On the front steps he shook his head and his long ears made a flapping sound. He sat down and began licking himself.

"That is the most disgusting thing I've ever seen in my life," Jamie told him, and closed the door. She turned for the kitchen, nodded once at Max, and made for the coffeepot. She was determined to act as though nothing had happened the night before.

"Your eyes don't look so good, Swifty," Max said.

"I didn't sleep well," she said, avoiding eye contact.

"I guess that makes two of us. I was wondering. Maybe I should drive you back to Beaumont. You'd be safer."

She turned and gaped. "No way. Not until we find out who killed Rawlins." She spied the newspaper in his hand. "Oh, damn."

"I went out earlier to get the paper. You made headlines, Swifty."

"That's why you want me to go back, isn't it? You're afraid somebody will recognize me."

"No. The picture isn't even close." He held it up. "See for yourself."

Jamie hurried over and studied the drawing. The wig made a lot of difference; bangs covered most of her forehead, giving her face a rounder look. The slightly upturned nose was close, but the eyes were all wrong. She drew a sigh of relief.

"Nobody is going to recognize you as this woman," Max said. "Did you give anyone your last name?"

Jamie shook her head. "Nobody asked. Not even Rawlins."

"Probably because you told him you had a sexual addiction." Max shook his head as though he still couldn't believe she'd done it. "Most people would want their anonymity protected. He would have been sensitive enough to know that."

She gave a shaky breath. "You're saying it's safe for me to go to Wal-Mart?"

He suddenly looked amused. "God forbid I try to stop you from shopping." His eyes took on a tender look. "If it helps to get out, I'll take you. You're safe as long as you're in a crowd."

She had wondered about what to do about meeting Michael for breakfast. "I'll be fine on my own."

He didn't argue. "You're not the only person the police are looking for. A bellboy is being questioned about a man who offered him one hundred bucks to borrow his clothes and push the food cart into Rawlins's room. Fortunately, Dave was in disguise as well." He paused. "We can continue using the name Trotter, and since Jane is such a common name, I don't see a problem there, either."

"Sounds like everything is going to be OK then."

"For the time being."

Jamie didn't miss the edge in his voice.

JAMIE SLID INTO THE BOOTH ACROSS FROM Michael Juliano. She stiffened when she noticed the folded newspaper beside him. She was just being paranoid, she told herself.

He smiled at her. "Good morning. Or is it?"

She froze. "What do you mean?"

"You look tired."

"I didn't sleep well last night."

"Does it have anything to do with that wedding band you're wearing? Not that it's any of my business, of course."

Jamie's stomach took a nosedive as she realized she was wearing the wedding band she had put on before meeting with Harlan the day before. She had been so upset she hadn't thought to remove it when she'd returned home and changed. She hadn't been wearing it when she first met Michael and she wanted to keep things consistent. In his paranoid state he might shut down to her.

She had gone and blown her chance. "I can explain it," she said.

He leaned back in the booth as though waiting.

TWELVE

JAMIE WAS THANKFUL THE WAITRESS HAD picked that particular moment to bring coffee and menus. She waited until the woman walked away.

"My husband and I are divorcing," she said.

"But you still wear his ring?"

Jamie stared at it. "I suppose I'm still trying to come to terms with it. I should take it off and I do sometimes."

Michael seemed to ponder it. "I really don't have a right to ask. I mean, we barely know each other, right? I just . . ." He paused and gave a rueful smile.

"What?"

"I found myself looking forward to seeing you today, so the ring was a big surprise. I don't remember seeing it yesterday, but then, I was upset at the time. I'm sorry I butted in. And I'm sorry that you're going through a bad time. I was married once, but it didn't work out."

He looked genuinely sad for her. Jamie glanced down. It wasn't easy lying to someone who was so nice, and it wasn't easy keeping secrets from Max. But she seemed to be doing a lot of that lately. She had even called Vera and spent ten minutes on the phone lying to her about what a great time she was having in Tennessee. Yeesh.

But she had a very good reason for all the subterfuge. She was trying to keep Vera from worrying, and she was trying to get information from Michael that might protect him and lead her and Max to Nick Santoni. A girl had to do what a girl had to do.

"Jane, are you all right?"

Jamie looked up. "We barely know each other, Michael, and the last thing I want to do is burden you with my problems. I was just trying to be a friend when I thought you needed one."

He didn't respond.

"Would you rather I go?" She held her breath. Leaving was the last thing she wanted to do. If she left now she would be empty-handed as far as information was concerned.

"Please stay."

Jamie tried to hide her relief as she took a sip of her coffee. "How are you?"

"My sister was buried yesterday afternoon in a private ceremony. As much as I hate to say it, I'm relieved to have it over with. I didn't like seeing her suffer, you know?"

The waitress took their order and left them. "So what are you going to do now?" Jamie asked.

Michael shrugged. "Take it one day at a time. I own several delis in Knoxville. I have to look after them."

Jamie leaned closer. "Have you had any more threats?"

Michael glanced around the restaurant. "I wish I hadn't told you. I plan to take care of that little problem tonight."

"What do you mean?"

"I'm going to tell the guy flat-out no. I'm going to hire security guards to watch my delis, and I'm going to the cops. I'd rather spend the money on that than paying off thugs to keep them from burning my places to the ground."

"You're actually meeting with one of them?"

He nodded. "Yeah. It won't take long to say screw off. Excuse my language."

Jamie's mind raced. Finally, she gave a sigh. "What is it?"

"Nothing. You'll think it's silly."

"What?"

"Michael, I was going to invite you to dinner tonight. I figured it would lift your spirits." She shrugged. "Mine, too."

"I'm sorry." He reached across the table and squeezed her hand. "I would have gladly accepted under different circumstances."

Jamie pondered it. She didn't want to sound pushy and risk blowing it, but if she didn't come up with some kind of plan she'd lose her chance altogether. "Maybe we could have dinner afterward. What time are you meeting with this, um, person?"

"Eight o'clock. But we're meeting in Knoxville."

"I know how to get to Knoxville."

He hesitated. "I suppose that'll work. I'm just going to meet him in a bar, tell him I'm not going to do business with him, then walk away."

"We could meet somewhere close, say around eight-thirty?"

Michael looked thoughtful. He reached for a

napkin and scribbled on it. "There's a quaint little Italian restaurant down the street from where I'll be. It's called Jeno's; you can't miss it. I'll meet you out front at eight-thirty."

"Great. I look forward to it."

They made small talk until their breakfast arrived, but Jamie's mind wasn't on the conversation. She was already forming a plan in her head.

"SO, WHO'S THE GUY?" MUFFIN ASKED AS soon as Jamie had pulled from the parking lot and turned onto the highway.

Jamie had not been expecting the question. "How'd you know?"

"Female intuition."

"You're a computer, Muffin."

"Whatever. So who is he?"

"His name is Michael; he's very nice and drives an awesome Jaguar. He's also going through a bad time, and he needs a friend right now. That's all we are, friends. We're having dinner tonight."

"Does Max know?"

Jamie sighed. "No, I haven't told him. But I'll have to; otherwise, he'll worry."

"You should go, Jamie. It'll do you good."

She looked at the dashboard. "Really?"

"That doesn't mean you don't need to take extra precautions, but you need to do something to take your mind off what happened yesterday. You haven't even had time to get over all the crap you went through in Beaumont."

"You worried I might crack up or something? That you might have to find me a quiet state-operated mental hospital?"

"I don't think you need to sit in that cabin night after night while Max and I try to break through the Santoni family's firewalls. Or listen to Dave," she added.

MAX'S JAW WENT SLACK IN DISBELIEF. "ARE you saying you have a date?"

Jamie pretended to fluff the throw pillows on the sofa so she didn't have to look at him. "No, it's not a date; I'm meeting this guy for dinner." She turned to Max. "He just lost his sister. She was his twin. He's devastated, and he needs somebody to talk to."

Max scooted his chair back from the kitchen table, where computers, monitors, and various other equipment that Jamie knew nothing about blinked and winked and made soft whirring sounds.

"You always find them, don't you, Swifty?"

"What do you mean?"

"You're just like my sister. The two of you must have radar. If somebody has problems, you lock in to them and you immediately have to fix whatever is wrong." Max suddenly looked suspicious. "How well do you know this person?"

"Well, I haven't had time to call a profiler from the FBI, but I managed to lift his prints off his water glass, so I should know something by the time we're supposed to meet."

Max didn't seem to find humor in her remark. "How do you know he wasn't just using a line?"

"Max, he asked me to look at his sister's dress, for God's sake. The one she was buried in yesterday. The man is in a lot of pain. I don't care if you think I'm just a big softie, I can't turn my back on him."

"Just be careful, OK? I know you need to get out, but don't forget what we're up against."

Which made her all the more determined to find out what Michael knew. *If* he knew anything, she reminded herself. And once she did, she would lay it all at Max's feet and have the inside edge to her story.

A buzzing sound from a speaker drew Max's attention away from her for a moment. "It's just Dave."

Dave came through the front door a few minutes later. He looked anxious. "I can't find the deer anywhere."

Max stared at the man.

"What deer?" Jamie asked.

Max spoke. "Dave swerved to miss a buck this morning, but now he has convinced himself he hit it."

"I could have nicked him," Dave said.

"I was in the truck when the deer ran out in front of you, Dave," Max went on. "You missed him by a mile. We've gone back to look for him twice. If you had hit him he'd be dead by the road."

"Not necessarily. He could have wandered off. He might be lying in a gully in pain at this very moment."

"Try not to think about it," Max said. "We have to worry about Jamie right now. She has a hot date tonight."

Dave looked at Jamie. "Man, you move fast."

Jamie rolled her eyes at Max. "Thanks."

Dave stepped closer to Max. "Are my eyes red?"

"They look perfectly fine to me."

"I can't remember if I took my allergy pill this morning. I should probably count them."

"Dave likes to count his pills," Max told Jamie. "And when he's not counting his pills he counts license tags and telephone poles."

Dave, who'd reached into his pants pocket for his prescription bottle, simply stood there. "It's what I do," he finally said. He glanced at Jamie. "Didn't your new boyfriend notice you were wearing a wedding ring?"

"It doesn't matter. Michael and I are going to have an affair anyway."

Max tried to hide his amusement. "They can't help themselves, Dave. They took one look at each other and their morals flew right out the window."

Dave didn't seem to be listening. "I should probably run down and take another look just to make sure that deer is OK."

Max stood. "I need to check in with Muffin."

Jamie watched him go, then sank onto the sofa. If only she could tell him what she thought she knew.

"That thing is covered with dust mites," Dave said.

Jamie just looked at him.

MAX CLIMBED INTO THE TRUCK. "HAVE YOU
got anything on Santoni yet?" he asked Muffin.

"Your timing is perfect. I just found Santoni's address."

"Damn, that's great news," Max said, grinning. "Just what we've been waiting for."

"His place is about forty-five minutes from
here. It would have been a whole lot easier
finding him if the man put things in his own
name, but like I said before, he has a number
of aliases."

"You have my undivided attention."

"The name Juliano has popped up a couple
of times in the family tree. It was Nick's
mother's maiden name; seems Nick borrows
from that tree now and then just to keep people
guessing. Nick's sister was named Bethany-
Ann Juliano Santoni, if you can believe it."

"I didn't know he had a sister. Nothing
we've pulled up mentioned siblings."

"I was playing around with birth records and
discovered Santoni's mother, Mary-Bethany
Elizabeth Juliano Santoni, gave birth to twins
in a hospital in Carlstadt, New Jersey. Michael
Nicholas and Bethany-Ann Juliano."

"That's interesting."

"Yeah, but this is where it gets weird. Bethany-Ann died at birth. That didn't stop Nick from borrowing. He's using the name Michael Juliano."

"What else?"

"I discovered Nick Santoni attended Saint Teresa's Holiness School in Carlstadt, New Jersey, but that was before computers, so I can't get anything more. He had a couple of best friends, Rudolf Marconi or Rudy, as they call him, and Thomas Peter Bennetti."

"I'm having trouble keeping up with all these names," Max said.

"Most of these guys are Catholics, and you often find their names contain one of the saints. Go figure. I've found various mortgages in and around Knoxville owned by a Michael Juliano. Marconi owns a couple of bars in Knoxville."

"What about the other guy? Bennetti."

"He sort of dropped out of the picture."

NICK SANTONI'S HOME WAS PERCHED HIGH ON a mountain and surrounded by a massive brick wall, the house built of stone and granite that had been dragged up the side of the mountain. Cameras sat atop the gated entrance, aimed in all directions. They were monitored by Santoni's employees, who watched from the office of a nearby building, which also housed a kennel of Doberman pinschers. Each hour, a man leashed two dogs and walked the property.

Nick pulled up to the gate, and in a matter of seconds it slid open. He parked in front of the house, unlocked the door, and went inside. The slate floors and heavy leather furniture had been designed for a man, and although Nick owned several properties in various locations, his mountain home was his favorite.

He strode purposefully toward a wet bar, poured his favorite scotch into a short glass, and drained it. His cell phone rang, but he ignored it. Instead, he poured a second scotch, sank into the nearest chair, and opened his newspaper. The headline stared back at him: *Renowned Evangelist Found Dead in Hotel Room.* Nick reread the article and tossed the paper aside. He leaned back in his chair and closed his eyes.

His cell phone rang again. With a sigh, he reached into the pocket of his slacks and pulled it out.

"You've been ignoring my calls," the voice said from the other end. It was the tired, raspy voice of a man who had spent much of his life smoking expensive cigars with his brandy. "Is that any way to treat your favorite uncle?"

"I was tied up most of the morning, Uncle Leo," Nick said. "I couldn't talk."

"I've been listening to the news, Nicholas."

"Yeah?"

"You want to tell me about it?"

"What? You think I killed Rawlins?"

"Not at first. Then I started playing around with it in my mind."

"You got it all wrong. I'm as surprised over his death as you are."

"You mean his murder." The man paused. "I have always been able to tell when you're lying, Nicholas. You lied about hiring Vito Puccini, and you're lying now. I sent you down there to protect you. I'd hoped you would change. You think you can just kill somebody, bury the body, and that's it? You think the cops are idiots? You watch too many gangster movies, Nicky. The family is sick of your tactics. You've become a problem. A big problem."

Nick frowned. "The family is always on my ass, trying to pin something on me. If someone in this town takes a shit, I'm the one who gets blamed for it."

"You've been stepping in shit all your life, kid. Problem is, you track it all over the place so that your family has to walk in it. The police watch our houses. My daughter can't take my grandchildren to the park because men follow her."

"What would I have to gain by killing Rawlins?" Nick asked.

"You're asking the wrong question."

"OK, what's the right question?"

"What would you have to lose if he lived?"

Nick sighed. "I don't have any answers, Uncle Leo. I've got my boys looking into it. That's the best I can do right now."

"Harlan Rawlins was the only thing you had going for you."

"That's not true! I've got money coming in from a number of sources."

"Yeah, but he was your big fish." Leo suddenly went into a fit of coughing. "I'm an old man, Nicky. I don't need this. The family doesn't need this. Losing that TV network was a bad mistake, and we still haven't recovered that loss. I can't help you anymore." He paused. "You need to come home."

Nick was silent for a moment. "What are you saying?" He wiped a hand down his face and found it wet. "Have I been replaced?"

"It's best this way."

"Look, Uncle Leo, I'm in the middle of

something down here, and I can't let go. I didn't want to say anything until I took care of it, but I've got Maximillian Holt and his girlfriend in the palm of my hand."

Silence.

"Max Holt has been snooping around, Uncle Leo. He somehow managed to trace Vito Puccini back here, so he found out Harlan hired him. Hell, Harlan even wrote a letter of recommendation."

"Which you forced him to do," the man said knowingly.

"I don't know what you're talking about."

"Harlan Rawlins wouldn't know how to go about hiring a hit man. Do you take me for an old fool?"

"You don't have to believe me, Uncle Leo, but I'm telling you Holt is bad news. Hell, he has more connections than we do. He could have easily taken Harlan out."

"Are you planning to kill again, Nicholas?" The man sounded tired.

"Holt could hurt the family, Uncle Leo. He could expose us all."

"The family has done nothing to Max Holt; you have. And when you kill him you will have to kill his girlfriend, and then there will be someone else. It never stops. You create too many problems."

"Listen to me, old man! Your grandchildren will *never* be able to play in the park as long as Max Holt is alive, because he's going to even the score."

"I think you are very confused," Leo said. "You are no match for a man like Max Holt. You are a coward. Your own father knew this."

Nick started to answer, but the line went dead.

THIRTEEN

DETECTIVE PETE SILLS SIPPED COFFEE FROM A chipped mug and waited until the lab technician finished speaking to another detective before he approached him. "Hey, Lance, you got anything for me on the Rawlins case yet?"

"Are you kidding? The chief has us working double-time on it. He obviously wants to look good in front of the media. When is his next press conference?"

Sills smiled. "You know I don't keep up with the politics around this place. I'm just a worker bee."

"You and me both," Lance said. "Anyway, we matched the pills they found on him, as well as those he'd stashed in his desk drawer, and it's obvious he came about them illegally, since the bottles were unmarked. This guy was taking a shitload of stuff. I'm surprised he could even remember what they were, or the dosage.

"I also ran a test on the powder they found beside the wine bottle, and the ingredients are consistent with those found in most laxatives."

"There was evidence he'd gotten sick shortly before his death," Sills said. "I wonder if maybe it was all that crap in his system."

Lance shrugged. "We won't know the facts until the autopsy, of course."

"I've talked to the wife," Sills said. "Rawlins's beatings sent her to the emergency room more than once."

"You think she killed him?"

"She had motive. Problem is, she can't weigh more than a hundred pounds, and she's a timid little thing. I just can't picture her killing her husband with a knife."

"Maybe she has a boyfriend."

Sills met his gaze. "It wouldn't have been easy. Harlan kept her in her bedroom most of the time."

"Sounds like he was one mean sonofabitch."

DAVE WAITED UNTIL MAX CLIMBED INTO THE
bucket that was attached to the hydraulic lift to
Bennett Electric's truck. "You got everything
you need?" he asked.

"Yea. Once I attach the recording transmitter, I'll hook into the telephone line and run a
test."

"Look, Max, I'd go up in the bucket if it
weren't for my vertigo."

"Naw, I personally want to get a look at Santoni's place."

Physically finding Santoni's house had been
no easier than Muffin getting the information
that the property wasn't listed to Nick Santoni.
Tom Bennett of Bennett Electric had been able
to locate property belonging to a Michael Juliano in his computer. He'd given Max a
county map and marked the area in red, but
many of the dirt roads leading to the residence
were unmarked. Max and Dave had combed
the mountain until they found the massive
brick wall that enclosed what appeared to be a
compound of sorts.

"Don't forget to take pictures," Dave said.
"Oh God, I hope we didn't forget the camera."

"I've already told you I've got it. Five times I've told you."

"Just want to make sure."

"Take me up."

Dave pressed a button, and the bucket rose slowly upward. Once Max was in position, he went to work. Soon it would be possible to access incoming and outgoing calls on Santoni's line.

JAMIE HAD SPENT THE DAY CLEANING THE cabin and working on her story, filling the pages of her notebook with her impressions of Rawlins and the town of Sweet Pea, as well as the faces she'd seen in the congregation. The bottom line: People needed hope, and Harlan Rawlins had given them that. Because so much money had come into his ministry he was able to make a difference in some ways, but he'd been more interested in lining his pockets and paying off those who were extorting money from him. Had he not been so greedy, had he not owed the mob hush money, Harlan Rawlins would have been able to make staggering changes with his ministry.

Jamie found herself wondering about the

man. Had he always been a phony? she mused.
Or had he started out with good motives, only
to be seduced by money? And what about ru-
mors of affairs and possible spousal abuse?
What did the mob have on Harlan that he'd
been willing to pay so much money to keep
quiet?

IT WAS AFTER 6:00 P.M. BY THE TIME MAX AND
Dave arrived back at the cabin. Jamie had
bathed and dressed in a white denim skirt and
navy knit top, minus the push-up bra. Her
blonde hair hung free, falling to her shoulders.

Max took one look at her and arched one
brow. "Wow. Your new friend is going to take
one look at you in that outfit and forget about
all his problems. Maybe I should go as a chaperon."

"I'm too old for a chaperon, Max, but thanks
just the same. Where have you guys been all
day?"

"Maybe you should sit down first," Dave
said, "because you're not going to believe it."

Jamie looked at Max. "Oh, yeah?" she said.

"We found Santoni's place," he told her.

Her jaw dropped. "For real?" She couldn't

hide the excitement in her voice. "What's it like?"

"Nice hideout," he said, "surrounded by what looks like the Great Wall of China."

Dave nodded. "Max attached a recording transmitter to his telephone line so we could monitor his calls."

"Wow, we're finally getting somewhere," she said. "Did you happen to get a look at Santoni?"

Max shook his head. He looked disappointed. "I wish. The place is under heavy guard. We had to do the job and get out so we wouldn't attract attention." He didn't look happy as he walked over to his laptop and sat down.

"We have pictures of his place," Dave said. "Or should I say his fortress." He handed Jamie several photos.

"Looks like a prison," she said.

"It's secure," Max told her as he checked his E-mail. "He's got almost as much security on his place as I do on mine. Of course, what I use is more sophisticated."

"Yeah, but you don't have a herd of Doberman pinschers walking the grounds," Dave said.

"I would love to know what Santoni looks

like," Jamie said. Even as she said it, she hoped she would get the opportunity later. She suspected Santoni was the one threatening Michael, but what she didn't know was whether he would show up personally to meet with Michael or send one of his men.

"What are you doing?" Jamie asked Max.

"Muffin is sending me what stats she has on Santoni. The reason we couldn't find anything at first is because he has everything in his sister's name and she's deceased."

"You're not thinking of trying to get into his place, are you?"

"There's no need," Max said. "We wouldn't find anything in his residence. That would make him vulnerable to possible search and seizure if he got busted. If the cops even know where he lives," he added. "I figure he's operating out of the back room of one of his businesses under an assumed name. Hopefully, we'll hear something in a phone conversation."

"What's next?"

"We're going to grab some gear and equipment and spend the night near Santoni's place," he said. "We have to be within range of the transmitter in order to tap in to his phone calls. Dave and I found a shack in the woods not far from the house. You can tell it hasn't been used in a while."

"It sounds dangerous."

"Damn right," Dave said. "The place is full of spiderwebs, not to mention . . ." He paused and glanced at Max. "Dust mites."

"Will you be spending the night out there?" Jamie asked. Not only was she anxious at the risk they were taking, but she also didn't relish the thought of being alone at night in the cabin.

"I'll take the first watch," Dave said. "No sense us both being there."

Max looked at Jamie. "I'll stay with Dave for a while and try to be back by the time you get home. You *are* coming back tonight, I assume." He gave her outfit another once-over.

Jamie tossed him a look. "Very funny. I should be home before midnight."

"That's kind of late, isn't it?"

"I'm not meeting him until eight-thirty."

"I hope he's not married, too," Dave said. When Max and Jamie looked at him, he shrugged. "I know you and Jamie aren't really married, but this guy she's going out with doesn't know it. What if he has a wife? What if she's the jealous type?"

"He's not married," Jamie said.

Max looked troubled. "Maybe you and I

should talk further before you meet this guy. I don't even know where the two of you are going."

"Would the two of you relax?" Jamie said. "I'm having dinner with the guy. He's probably going to want to talk about his sister. I'm going to listen to him, try to be supportive, and then I'm coming home." That wasn't all she was going to do, but that's all she was going to tell them for the moment. She hoped when she left Michael Juliano she would have big news for Max. A name or a face.

"Would you mind driving Bennett's truck tonight?" Max asked. "I'd like to have Muffin around."

"No problem."

JAMIE HAD TO STOP AND ASK FOR DIRECTIONS twice, but she finally managed to find the Italian restaurant Michael had told her about. The sun was setting. She searched the area and found a small sports bar located within a block of the restaurant.

She parked in a side alley and waited. She did not wish to be seen by Michael. She had no idea if he planned to meet his party at that particular bar; all she could do was wait and watch for any sign of him.

The streetlights flickered on, but Jamie was hidden in shadows. She hoped a policeman didn't drive by and find her illegally parked, because she would have a difficult time explaining why she was there.

Shortly before eight, Jamie spied Michael's Jaguar. She instinctively ducked, then remembered he couldn't see her. She raised the binoculars she'd found beneath the front seat; obviously Max and Dave had used them earlier. She could see Michael's car perfectly, but she could barely make out his profile in the dark interior. She watched him select a parking place near the door of the bar. He pulled into the vacant slot and waited. Jamie waited as well.

The minutes ticked by slowly. Jamie drummed her fingers on the steering wheel and hummed a tune under her breath. A black Jeep Cherokee pulled into the parking lot and a couple emerged, young and smiling.

Jamie sighed and shifted in the seat. What if the person Michael was meeting had arrived early? For all she knew the man could have been inside sipping cold beer and watching a sports program on TV before she got there. Maybe she was on a wild-goose chase.

Jamie perked up as a silver SUV pulled into the parking lot. She put the binoculars to her eyes and followed the vehicle. The driver chose a slot near Michael's. Jamie watched him climb from the SUV, but it was hard to get a good look at his face in the dim light. His hair was long and dark and hung in what looked like a ponytail down his back. As he started for the front door of the bar, Michael climbed from his Jaguar.

She waited until they were both inside before she grabbed a flashlight and her notepad and climbed from the truck. She hurried toward the parking lot and to the SUV; then, checking to make sure nobody was around, she turned on the flashlight and shone it through the back window. All at once, something hit the glass hard. Jamie's heart gave a lurch, and she cried out as two angry-looking Doberman pinschers pressed their faces against the window, teeth bared, snarling and barking as though they could come through the glass with very little trouble.

Their barks were deafening. She had to get away before they drew attention to her. Jamie quickly copied down the license tag number. She stood and turned.

She was face-to-face with the longhaired man.

"What do you think you're doing?" he said,

his voice barely audible among the barking dogs.

Jamie felt a chill race up her spine as she stared into the flat, emotionless eyes of the man before her. They were as black as his long braided hair, as black as the slacks and silk shirt he wore. Was it Nick Santoni? He looked like a mobster. She felt a sudden adrenaline rush.

"I asked you a question," he said.

There was nobody around; the sky seemed to have darkened considerably in the past few minutes. Jamie knew she needed a damn good answer. "What the hell does it look like I'm doing?" she said, trying to make herself heard over the barking dogs. "I'm copying down this license tag number. You got a problem with that?"

"This is my vehicle."

"No way. I know who this SUV belongs to."

From his pocket, the man pulled a key ring, a small black object attached to it. He pressed it, and there was a bleeping sound. Jamie knew he had just unlocked the door. Probably planned to shove her inside and take off, she thought. He wouldn't have to shoot her; the dogs would kill her instantly.

Shit.

The man opened the driver's door and reached inside for a pack of cigarettes. He shouted at the dogs, and they grew quiet.

"I guess this is your vehicle," Jamie said. "I thought it, um, belonged to someone else."

His gaze was unflinching. Jamie knew it would be so easy for him to put a gun to her head and order her in. Max would have no idea what had happened.

"I thought it belonged to the woman my husband is seeing," she said at last. "I don't know much about vehicles, but this looks exactly like hers. Only I don't think she has dogs."

In one easy move, he snatched Jamie's notepad from her hand, tossed it into the front seat, and closed the door. He hit the automatic lock before she could protest.

"Hey, give that back," she said. "It has all my information in it."

He turned and started for the bar. The dogs were barking again. Jamie panicked. The last thing she needed was for Nick Santoni or one of his men to have her notes in his possession. "Wait a minute!" she called out. "You can't just take my notepad!"

He lit a cigarette and blew the smoke in her face. "Report me to the police if you like," he said, "but stay the hell away from my vehicle."

He gave her a long silent look before walking away.

"Dammit!" Jamie said aloud. What was she going to do now? She couldn't very well break into the vehicle; the dogs would eat her alive before she reached her notepad. Without wasting another second, she hurried across the street toward Bennett's truck. It wasn't until she was safely inside with the doors locked that she realized she should have at least checked the license tag again and written it down when she got into the truck. She tried to remember the numbers but couldn't. She couldn't risk going back over, even in her truck. If Michael saw her he would suspect something was up.

JAMIE MET MICHAEL IN FRONT OF JENO'S AT precisely 8:30. He smiled and gave her a hug. "Where'd you park?" he asked.

She pointed. "I'm over there. My truck was giving me trouble, so I borrowed one from a friend."

"A *male* friend?" Michael said, arching both brows. "Should I be jealous?"

"My friend is happily married." Jamie was surprised he could be so jovial after meeting with someone who had probably just threatened him with extortion. "Are you OK?"

"Uh? Oh, yes, it has all been taken care of."

"What do you mean, it has been taken care of?"

"I told him I would go to the police if he came around again."

Jamie just stared. People like Nick Santoni weren't afraid of the police. She was about to say as much when he changed the subject.

"You know, when you're ready to trade in that relic of yours, I might be able to help you find a good deal on a car. I have a friend in the business."

"Fleas loves that old truck," she said.

"Maybe you could buy him a new truck. I hope you're hungry. This restaurant has great food. I'd love to own the place, but Jeno wants to keep it in the family, you know, husband and wife team. He's struggling to make ends meet, poor fellow."

Jamie noted the line that started inside and wound its way out. "It looks packed to me."

"Yes, but his overhead is high, and he has trouble with vandals. This is not a great neighborhood. And to tell you the truth, I don't think he and his wife are good business managers. I could really turn a profit in a place like this."

"I hope you made reservations."

"We don't need them." He offered his arm, and Jamie took it. He led her inside, where the air hung heavy with the smell of garlic, Italian sausage, and baked bread. Waitresses bustled about in peasant-style uniforms, and a short balding man was frantically cleaning the only empty table available.

"Wait right here," Michael said. "I'm going to talk to Jeno." He walked over to the man, leaned forward, and spoke close to his ear. Jeno immediately stopped what he was doing and looked up. He nodded curtly at Michael.

"Jeno is clearing our table now," Michael said, rejoining Jamie.

She felt his hand at the small of her back, felt him prod her forward. "But what about those people waiting in line?"

"I'd ask them to join us, but there's no room."

Jamie could literally feel the heated stares as Jeno seated them and handed her a menu. "Thank you," she said. His gaze met hers. He was not a happy man. He walked away without a word.

Michael touched her hand. "You look so serious; what's wrong?"

Jamie shrugged. Perhaps she was being overly sensitive, but she could almost feel the hostility in the room. "I guess I'm feeling weird for taking the only available table. I wouldn't have minded waiting."

"Jeno was happy to oblige us, Jane. Now, if this were my place, there would be no waiting line. I'd expand."

"I like the quaintness," Jamie said. "It's so cozy." Jamie noticed several windows along one side had been boarded over. "What happened there?"

"Like I said, this isn't a great neighborhood. Two weeks ago, someone broke the windows. Jeno hasn't been able to afford to fix them because something happened to his walk-in freezer. He's closed on Sunday and Monday, so he walked in Tuesday morning to the smell of rotting meat. I'm sure that set him back. I offered to help, but he's a proud man, so what can I do?" He took a sip of water. "But I'll tell you this: For the right price I'd take this off his hands."

MAX WATCHED THE REARVIEW MIRROR AS they turned off the highway and took a series of dirt roads that led to Santoni's place. It was shortly after nine; the sun had finally disappeared behind the mountains.

Max took the road almost directly across from Santoni's. He cut his headlights, stopped, and waited until Dave climbed from the truck.

"This place is probably crawling with rattlesnakes," Dave muttered. "Did you know diamondback rattlesnakes have been known to reach lengths of eight feet?"

"Good thing you're wearing steel-toed work boots," Max said.

Dave quietly closed the door.

"Are we there yet?" Muffin asked.

"Yeah. Dave is going to lead the way with the flashlight. I figure the less light the better."

"How dangerous is this?" Muffin asked.

"It's far enough away from Santoni's that nobody should venture this way. If we were any farther we wouldn't be within range of the transmitter."

Max followed Dave down a narrow road and parked beside the ramshackle cabin. He climbed from the truck and picked up a box containing the equipment while Dave pulled out his backpack and other gear. He fastened a mask over his face before stepping through the cabin door. Inside, Max lit a lantern, and they went to work.

"You need to get out of here," Dave said,

his voice muffled behind the mask. "I can do the rest."

Max looked at him. "I should probably stay with you."

"I'm more concerned about dust mites than I am Santoni or his men showing up. Now get out of here and let a genius do his work."

RUDY MARCONI PARKED HIS SUV IN FRONT OF Nick's house. He had made the drive back from Knoxville in record time, even though it would have been difficult for most drivers to concentrate on the winding mountain roads with two Dobermans pacing the back restlessly. But Rudy kept the dogs with him at all times. They were young and still in training, but he was patient where his dogs were concerned.

That's where his patience ended. He was as hotheaded as Nick could be at times, which was why they understood each other so well and why their friendship had lasted for so many years.

Rudy climbed from the SUV and stretched. Dressed all in black, he was not easy to make out in the dark, and he liked it that way. He was better able to move about the property unseen. As Nick's head lieutenant and most devoted friend and employee, Rudy saw that things ran smoothly, in both Nick's personal and professional life. He reached beneath the seat for his gun and tucked it into the waistband of his slacks.

He went to the back of the SUV and lifted the tailgate. Once he'd leashed the dogs, he grabbed a flashlight and led them to the gate. He muttered a few words into the speaker, and it slid open.

He crossed the highway and followed the path that led through the woods on the other side. The dogs pulled at the leash as though sensing something was about to happen. Some minutes later, he came upon the cabin. He stared for a moment at the window and the faint glow coming from inside.

Rudy reached for his gun. Very quietly he walked toward the cabin. He aimed the gun and kicked open the door.

Dave jumped as the door to the cabin burst open and a man stepped inside. Dave's eyes traveled quickly from the gun to the dogs. He removed his headset.

"Well now," Rudy said, "what have we got here?" He stepped closer. He raised his eyes to

Dave, and they locked gazes. Rudy aimed his gun and fired three shots.

Dave dived to the floor as the equipment literally burst all around him. He grabbed a chair leg and raised it chest high in an attempt to defend himself.

Rudy laughed, aimed his gun once more, and fired off another shot. The chair leg splintered. He laughed at Dave, reached down, and unleashed one of the dogs.

Dave cried out as the Doberman sank his teeth into his thigh.

FOURTEEN

It was approaching eleven-thirty when Jamie insisted that Michael take her back to her truck. After she ate her fill at Jeno's—antipasto salad, manicotti stuffed with spinach and ricotta, and a side dish of steamed zucchini—Michael had driven her in his car to a twenty-four-hour bakery for his favorite cannoli and freshly brewed coffee. Afterward, he'd taken her by one of his delis. Jamie had begun to get bored while touring the meat counter.

She began to think the date would never end. Not only did Michael seem intent on dragging out the evening to the next presidential election, but he also was getting clingy. Jamie did not like clingy.

Michael, having reluctantly agreed to drive

her back, had just fastened his seat belt when his cell phone rang. He checked the number before he answered. "Yes?" He listened.

Jamie saw the change in him instantly. His face hardened, and his knuckles turned white on the steering wheel.

Finally, he spoke. "I'll deal with it later," he said and hung up.

"Is something wrong?" Jamie asked.

"Nothing I can't handle." He smiled at her, but it didn't reach his eyes. "Anybody ever tell you that you worry too much?" He drove in the direction of Jeno's, where she had parked Bennett's truck. After remaining silent for a moment he placed his hand on hers. "You're awfully quiet. As a matter of fact, you've been quiet most of the night. Did you not have a good time?"

"I guess I've got a lot on my mind," she said. "And I did enjoy myself. Thanks for a nice evening."

"Hey, you took me out, remember?"

Jamie tried not to think of why she had actually invited him out, because that would only remind her how dismally she had failed. "Then you should be thanking me," she said after a moment. And there was something about Michael that left her uneasy. It had all started

when he'd jumped to the head of the line at
the restaurant.

She did not like people who butted in line.
She had hated it as far back as grammar school
when Iva-Jean Tidwell used to butt in front of
her while playing kickball. The teacher had insisted on doing everything, including going to
the bathroom, in alphabetical order, but either
Iva-Jean had forgotten that the letter *S* for *Swift*
came before the letter *T* for *Tidwell* or she was
just plain rude. It wasn't until the last year in
fourth grade that Jamie had finally stood up to
Iva-Jean, and there had been some serious butt-
kicking as a result. In the end, they had both
been suspended from school for three days for
fighting.

"I'd like to see you again, Jane," Michael
said, interrupting Jamie's thoughts.

"That's nice," Jamie said, even though it
wasn't what she wanted to hear. She supposed
part of it was her disappointment in not knowing the identity of the person he'd met with
earlier and losing her opportunity to get the
license tag number. Not only that, she'd lost
her notebook that contained valuable information and it was in the possession of someone
who might be dangerous to her and Max.

"So what do you say?" Michael asked.

Jamie knew she should be flattered. Michael was handsome and successful, and he drove a nice car. In Beaumont that was reason enough to marry after the first date. It was also to his advantage that he did not have plywood nailed to the front floorboard so that Jamie didn't have to fear falling through the floor each time they hit a bump.

"I like you, Michael," she said, "but I'm very confused right now. I had no right to invite you out while I'm in the middle of divorce proceedings."

"I could be a good friend to you at a time like this."

Jamie suspected he had more than mere friendship on his mind. She knew what the problem was, of course. She had started comparing men to Max, and they always fell short.

The streets were dark and deserted when they passed Jeno's. Michael pulled behind Bennett's truck. "I don't like the idea of your driving all the way back to Sweet Pea this late at night," he said, gazing at her in the semi-darkness of the car.

"I'll be fine."

Once again, he reached for her hand. "You

know, we don't have to say good night. You could come to my place."

"I can't."

"Because of your husband?"

"My life is complicated."

"Then why don't you allow me to make a few decisions for you?" He smiled and hit the automatic lock.

MAX CHECKED HIS WRISTWATCH AGAIN. MID-night. He looked at Fleas. "Your mistress is late." The dog whimpered and sank to the floor. Max walked over to the hound and gazed down at him. Finally, he knelt beside the animal and petted him. "I'm sure she's fine."

The dog sat up, yawned, and stretched.

"What I'd like to know is what we're supposed to do in the meantime." Max picked up some printouts, only to toss them aside. Fleas walked over to him. "What do you say we pop the top on a cold one and find us a wrestling channel?"

The dog thumped his tail against the floor.

Max walked to the refrigerator and opened the door. "First, we need to get some food into us. I don't know about you, but I'm hungry." Fleas joined him at the door and stared.

"You like cold cuts?" Max asked, pulling out a package of sliced ham. He opened the pack, pulled off a piece for himself and one for the dog. Fleas swallowed his in one quick gulp. Next, Max reached for the cheese. "This is what I like about eating at the refrigerator," he told the eager dog. "No dirty dishes to clean up afterward." He held the cheese high and Fleas jumped for it.

"Hello!" Max shouted. "Would you look at that!"

The dog wagged his tail as Max pulled out another slice of cheese.

"Ready?"

Fleas barked.

Max tossed the slice in the air, and Fleas jumped and caught it in his mouth once more. Max laughed. "I'm going to tell Jamie I taught you how to do that."

Once they'd finished snacking, Max grabbed a beer, twisted off the top, and took a sip. He walked over to the coffee table, picked up the remote control, and turned on the TV. He sat down on the sofa. Fleas climbed up beside him and propped his big head in Max's lap.

"Does your mother allow you on the furniture?" he asked.

Fleas closed his eyes and began to snore.

JAMIE WONDERED WHAT KIND OF GAME MI-
chael was playing. The hair on the back of her
neck prickled. Not a good sign. She straightened in the seat. "Look, it's late, and I'm
tired." And annoyed, she wanted to add. She
didn't like this gnawing feeling in the pit of
her stomach. "So stop kidding around and let
me out of the car."

"You could sleep in my guest room if you
preferred. Tomorrow I would prepare you a
nice breakfast."

"Michael, I—"

"What if I said I wasn't going to take no for
an answer?"

Jamie felt a trickle of unease run down her
spine. She looked at him. His expression was
hard to read; she could not tell whether he was
serious or merely playing a bad joke on her.
"Maybe some other time, but not tonight."

"Jane?"

She reached for the handle. "Unlock the car,
please." When he didn't make a move to do
so, she turned to face him, but she was suddenly blinded by a set of headlights. A patrol
car pulled up beside them with two officers in-

side. Michael pushed a button, and his window slid down silently.

"You folks having a problem?" the officer on the driver's side asked.

Michael smiled. "I'm trying to talk my date into a good night kiss, but she seems reluctant."

The two policemen looked at each other and grinned. Finally, the driver nodded at Jamie. "It's after midnight, lady, and this neighborhood ain't so great. Why don't you give the poor guy a good night kiss so y'all can be on your way?"

Jamie couldn't deny the relief she felt as she gazed across at the smiling patrolmen. "Well, OK." She leaned across the seat and gave Michael a peck of a kiss on his lips. "Satisfied?"

"Oh, man, that's really lame," one of the officers said.

Michael turned to them. "I would probably have gotten a better one if you guys hadn't shown up."

"Would you please let me out of the car now?" Jamie asked.

Michael chuckled but hit the automatic lock. Jamie opened her door. "I'll follow you back to Sweet Pea," he said.

She met his gaze, her own cool. Inside, she

was furious. "Good night, Michael," she said, trying to talk around clenched teeth. She already had her keys in her hand by the time she reached Bennett's truck. She unlocked the door, jerked it open, and, in a fit of temper, tossed her purse on the passenger seat as hard as she could. It bounced and landed on the floor. She climbed into the truck, punched the lock down, and started the engine. The policemen waved at her as she pulled away.

Jamie didn't sigh a breath of relief until she turned onto the interstate, but she was conscious of Michael's headlights in her rearview mirror, could see the anxiety in her own eyes each time she glanced into the mirror and caught her own reflection.

It was then that she noted the gas gauge, the needle creeping toward empty. Shit. She'd been in such a hurry earlier to reach Knoxville that she'd completely forgotten to stop for gas. She flinched when the warning light came on. She glanced up just as an exit sign came into view, but there was no time to slow and pull off. Michael was right on her tail.

"Dammit!" she said.

The interstate held very little traffic, with the exception of a few 18-wheelers. The Sweet Pea exit was twenty miles away, and once she took it, there was a lone highway and a series of back roads before she reached the cabin. The gnawing in her stomach worsened.

Michael's Jaguar closed in on her.

Jamie suddenly remembered her cell phone. She automatically reached toward the seat beside her, only to find it empty. She glanced over. Her purse was lying on the floor, flush against the passenger door, where it had fallen when she'd thrown it on the seat too hard.

Jamie felt the truck swerve, and she gripped the steering wheel with both hands. She shot another glance at her purse. She would never be able to reach it. She would have to stop the truck and put it into gear, then lean across the other seat to put her hands on her purse. Bennett's truck was so big she needed both hands on the wheel.

Another exit sign came into view. Jamie read it quickly. There was a Waffle House in one direction and a campground in the other. No gas station. She passed the turnoff, watching the gas needle. Michael's headlights glared at her; he'd obviously turned on his high beams.

It seemed as though she had been driving forever when Jamie spied the tall Exxon sign in the distance. She glanced at the needle, kept

driving. When the exit sign appeared she didn't
bother to turn on her blinker, she just swerved,
and the truck barreled down the ramp. Behind
her Michael tapped his horn twice and continued on.

"Have a nice life, creep," Jamie said as she
drove toward the gas station. "You just saw the
last of me."

MAX JUMPED AT THE SOUND OF A VEHICLE
pulling in. He glanced at Fleas, who was still
snoring. "Some watchdog you are." He got up
and started for the door just as Jamie came in.

"Oh, hi," she said, trying to hide her relief
at seeing him. "Were you watching TV?"

"Yeah."

She just stood there for a moment, staring at
Max and thinking he had never looked so
good.

"Is something wrong?" he asked.

"I'm just glad to be home. Well, you know,
here."

"Glad to see you, too, Swifty."

Fleas got up and crossed the room. Jamie
petted him, and he nudged her with his nose.
"Hello, boy," she said.

"Actually . . ." Max paused and glanced at

his watch. "I was starting to wonder where you were."

Jamie raised her eyes to his. "I'm sorry I worried you." He didn't know the half of it, she thought.

"I've also been waiting for Dave to call." Max scratched the back of his head as though he didn't know what to say. "I was, uh, just about to make coffee."

"At this hour?"

"I really should wait up in case Dave calls."

Jamie tried to move, but Fleas had her pinned to her spot. "Excuse me, please." He raised his head and gave her a sad look.

"I think he missed you," Max said. "I tried to entertain him, but, well, I can only sit in the back of the truck with him for so long." He smiled.

"You haven't been feeding him junk food, have you?"

"No, we both had a nice garden salad for dinner."

Jamie regarded the dog. "You ate people food," she accused.

As though realizing he'd been caught, Fleas slid to the floor and covered his face with his paws. Jamie stifled a grin. "I knew it."

She and Max exchanged smiles. She took a

deep breath. She knew she had to come clean with him. "I have something to tell you."

"Uh-oh. You didn't wreck Bennett's truck, did you?"

"No, nothing like that," she said quickly. "Uh, Max, I should have told you this earlier, but I was afraid you'd get involved in it and—"

"Involved in what?"

"Well, one of the reasons I've been seeing this Michael person is because—"

"Oh, great, you're about to tell me you like this guy, is that it?"

Jamie shook her head. "No. Michael had something I wanted, Max."

Max's gaze slid from her head to her toes. "Maybe it was the other way around."

"Information, Max," Jamie said. "I thought Michael could give me information on Santoni."

"What?"

"You're not going to like it."

"Tell me anyway."

"I think I may have seen Santoni or one of his men tonight."

Max gaped at her. Finally, he crossed his arms over his wide chest. "You've got some explaining to do, Jamie."

"Promise not to get mad?"

"Start talking."

Jamie told him everything, about meeting Michael, his insinuations that someone from the mob was trying to extort money from him, everything. Max's frown deepened with every word. "I knew Michael was meeting the person tonight, so I made it a point to be nearby. I wanted to get a license tag number. I figured we could get Muffin to run a check on it and find out more. Only the guy caught me writing down his tag number and took my notepad away from me."

"Dammit!" Max yelled the word so loud that Fleas skittered beneath the kitchen table.

"Now look what you've done!" Jamie cried. She started for the table.

"Oh, no, you don't." Max grabbed her wrist and brought her to an abrupt halt. "Fleas is going to be OK, but you're in a shit load of trouble."

"I knew you wouldn't take this well," she said.

"Are you crazy! Why would you take a chance like that?"

"I wanted to help."

"Jesus Christ, I can't believe you'd do something so . . . so insane!" Max released her and began to pace. "God, Jamie, what if something had happened to you?"

"I'm sorry, Max. I know it sounds dumb, but I thought maybe—"

"What did you think, Jamie? That you could take on the mob by yourself?"

"Of course not. I was very careful. But I got a look at the guy, Max. It could have been Santoni himself. He's dark, and he's got long black braided hair. I know it's not much, but it might be something."

"I don't care," Max said, his tone still loud. "It wasn't worth the risk." He raked his hands through his hair, then paused as though just remembering he'd had most of it cut off.

"I was just trying to follow a lead," Jamie said. "I'm sorry that I don't have more for you."

"That is the absolute *least* of my concerns. This is *exactly* why I didn't want you to come with me." He turned away from her.

Jamie stepped closer. "I'm sorry."

Max kept his back to her. "How do you know the guy didn't follow you home?"

"It happened before I met Michael for dinner. I wasn't followed. It would have been easy to spot someone tailing me on these mountain roads. I kept checking." Which was true. She'd watched her rearview mirror closely after she'd gassed up and hit the road again.

"Did it occur to you what it would do to me if something happened to you?"

Jamie touched his shoulder. "Max?"

Without warning, he turned, took her hand in his, and pulled her into his arms.

Stunned, Jamie opened her mouth. Max took it as an invitation and covered it with his own. He pulled her tighter against him so that her body was flush against his. He cupped his palm at the back of her head, holding her in place, as the kiss became even more demanding. He raised back. "Promise me that you won't ever do something like that again."

"I promise."

He buried his face in her neck, inhaled her scent. He held her for a long time. "Dammit, Jamie, I want you so much it hurts."

"I feel the same."

Max raised his head and studied her. "Are you sure?"

She nodded.

"You just bought yourself a whole lot of trouble, Swifty." And he pushed her down the short hall to the bedroom.

FIFTEEN

THEY FELL TOGETHER ON THE BED, HARD. TOO
hard. The bed shifted and shook, the pillows
flew in every direction, and there was a loud
bam. To Jamie, it sounded as if the house had
caved in. She peeked out from beneath a pillow. The head- and footboards were still in
place, but the mattress and box spring were on
the floor. The bottom of the bed was still in
place, as though suspended. She blinked at the
sight. "We broke the bed."

"Ignore it," Max said, pressing his lips to
hers.

She kissed him back, even as their bodies
inched toward the top of the bed. Jamie's skull
touched the wall beneath the headboard. "I'm

a little uncomfortable," she said against Max's hot mouth.

He scooted her away from the wall. "Don't think about it. Don't think at all. You know what happens every time you start thinking."

Jamie slipped her arms around his neck, pulling him against her as she opened her mouth under his. It didn't matter that her feet were elevated a good eighteen inches above her head.

Max kissed her deeply, slipping his tongue into her mouth, exploring. She was only vaguely aware that Fleas was standing beside the bed sniffing her hair. Damned if Max didn't taste better than anything she had ever put in her mouth. Better than cotton candy and buttered popcorn. He broke the kiss, and they both sucked in air.

He looked into Jamie's eyes. "Are you OK?"

"I'm thinking this must be how it feels to be a bat. They hang upside down, too."

"See? You're doing it. You're thinking."

"I'll stop." Jamie put two fingers together, touched her temple, and turned them, as though switching off a button.

Max grinned and reclaimed her mouth. Jamie grasped his head, pulling him even closer. He paused only long enough to run his lips over her face, her closed eyelids, and her throat. She shivered.

Max pressed his lower body against hers. "You make me crazy," he said. "One minute I want to wring your neck, and the next minute I want to make love to you until we both drop."

He was making her crazy, too. Jamie reached for the buttons on his shirt. Her hands shook; her fingers trembled. She fumbled with the buttons, but her fingers were made clumsy by the need building inside of her. She could feel his skin beneath the shirt, solid and warm, but damned if she could get the buttons open. Finally, in a fit of frustration, she yanked the front of the shirt hard. Several buttons popped off and hit the floor.

They paused and watched the buttons bounce. "This was never my favorite shirt," Max said, covering her mouth once more.

Everything seemed to be happening quickly. Jamie was only vaguely aware of Max removing her sandals, caressing her legs. She reached for his belt as he slipped his hands up her skirt and tugged at her panties. Oh God, she thought as he managed to work them down past her hips and thighs and calves.

"Damn belt," she muttered, trying to unfasten it.

"You've got sexy legs," Max said, pressing his lips against her inner thigh.

"Thank you," she managed.

"You're welcome." He looked at her strangely. "Are you OK?"

"Maybe we could rearrange ourselves. My ears are pounding. I thought it was desire at first, but I think the blood is rushing to my brain."

In one move, Max turned her so that her head was at the foot of the bed and her feet at the top. "That's better," she said.

Max didn't seem to be listening. He shoved her skirt high as he kissed his way up her leg. He touched her lightly with his tongue, and Jamie cried out. She thought she heard Fleas moan in the background.

Fleas began to howl.

Max raised his head. "Come with me, Fleas," he said sternly.

The dog followed him from the bedroom and into the kitchen, where Max pulled out an entire package of ham. He tossed it, wrapper and all, to the floor before hurrying back into the bedroom, where he closed the door and locked it.

"Fleas is having a snack," he said, his gaze flitting over Jamie's half-clad body. He reached for his zipper. From somewhere far away a phone rang.

Jamie blinked rapidly, trying to clear her head, even as she reached for him. She barely choked the word, "Phone!"

Max paused, gave his head a shake, and raced from the room. He found his cell phone on the table. He pushed a button. "Yeah?" His breathing was ragged.

"Max Holt?"

"Speaking."

"Hello, Max. This is Nicholas Santoni."

JAMIE GOT OFF THE BED, PULLED HER SKIRT into place, and walked into the living room, where she found Max on his cell phone.

The look on his face told her something was wrong. "I'm listening," Max said.

Jamie waited, afraid to speak. Fleas got up and ambled toward them. Finally, Max hung up.

"What is it?" Jamie asked, almost afraid to hear the answer.

"That was Nick Santoni. He has Dave."

"What? Oh, my God! Is Dave—"

"He's alive, but he's hurt. One of Santoni's dogs got him."

"Oh, no!" Jamie covered her face.

Max rubbed his brow as he punched several buttons on his phone.

Jamie looked at Max. "How did Santoni know where to reach you?"

"He called from Dave's cell phone. My number is programmed into it. Our phones have a GPS, you know, a global positioning—"

"I know, it allows you to see where the two of you are calling from."

"Yeah, only I can't get a fix on his location, so the system has obviously been disabled." It was obvious Max was trying to remain calm. "I need blankets and clean sheets. Just in case."

"What? Why?"

"Find them, Jamie. Quick!"

She raced to the hall closet and began pulling out bed linen while Max threw on a T-shirt and grabbed his shoes. He stuffed his cell phone into his pocket.

"Please tell me what's going on," Jamie said as he took the bedclothes from her.

"Santoni is going to call me back in ten minutes and tell me where he dumped Dave. I don't know what kind of shape he'll be in, but I may have to put him in the back of the truck and take him to the hospital."

"Let me grab my shoes and purse," Jamie said as Max started for the door.

"You can't come."

Jamie stopped in her tracks.

"Santoni told me to come alone or not at all."

"Max, you can't—"

"I have no choice." He raced out the door without closing it.

"We should call the police!" she cried.

"No! Santoni will kill Dave for sure then."

Jamie watched in silence as Max wrenched open the door to the passenger's side of the truck, dumped the sheets and blankets on the seat, and slammed the door. "I'll call you when I know something."

Jamie watched him speed away. She stood there, staring out into the night, wondering what to do next. What was Santoni up to? she wondered, unable to come up with an answer that didn't scare her to death. Had he already killed Dave? Was he just reeling Max in so he could kill him as well? Her thoughts terrified her.

She closed the door, stood there for a moment, unable to think. She needed to do something. Should *she* call the police? And tell them what? She raked her hands through her hair. What to do, what to do?

Calm down, she told herself. She had to find something to do, something that would give her direction. She was usually pretty good in emergencies; it wasn't until afterward that she went ballistic. Coffee. That was always a good place to start. She needed to be alert when Max called.

She put on the coffee and then shoved a load of laundry into the washing machine just to have something else to do. She hated the washing machine because it was so loud. No telling how old it was. No time to worry about that now. She wondered how long she would have to wait before Max called. She would have to be ready to walk out the door the minute she heard from him. She had to be prepared in case—

She tried to think. She might have to meet Max at the hospital. If Dave was hurt, Max would definitely rush him to the hospital. That's probably when he would call her. She should change clothes. Better yet, a quick shower in case they had to sit with Dave a long time. Jamie hurried into her bedroom, grabbed a pair of slacks, a blouse, and fresh underwear, and raced into the bathroom.

. . .

Max's cell phone rang, and he snatched it up. "Hello, Max," Nick said from the other end of the line. His voice was smooth and unhurried, as though he had all the time in the world.

"How is Dave?" Max said.

"He's alive if that's what you're asking. Listen, I hear you're a genius. Let's see how smart you are. I'm going to give you a clue, and it's up to you to figure out where your friend is. If you do, he lives. If you fail, he dies."

"You're going to pay for this, Santoni."

"You have a choice, Holt. You play along or I disconnect our call and you will never find your friend. What's it going to be?"

"What's the clue?"

"Clue number one: Where do dead things go?"

"A funeral home? A morgue?"

Santoni chuckled. "Why are you asking me? I already know the answer. It's up to you to figure it out. Good luck, Max." The line went dead.

Max slammed the ball of his hand against the steering wheel. "Dammit!"

"I heard," Muffin said.

"Dave could be lying in a graveyard," Max said. "How many are there in this damn town?"

"I don't think so," Muffin said. "Did you not listen to the question? Santoni specifically asked where dead *things* go. *Things,* not *people.*"

"What things?" Max demanded.

"I don't know; I'm trying to figure it out."

"Oh, shit, I just thought of something."

"What?"

"Jamie could be in danger!"

IT WASN'T UNTIL SHE'D LATHERED HERSELF from head to toe that Jamie realized she'd forgotten to bring in her cell phone. Oh, crap. She quickly rinsed, wrapped a towel around her, and hurried into the living room for her purse. The phone wasn't there. Where had she left it? She began to search. Had she left the thing in the truck?

She dressed in record time. The telephone rang in the kitchen and Jamie raced for it. Max was on the other end.

"Jamie, get out of the house!"

Her heart lurched. "What? What's wrong? Have you got Dave?"

"No, I'm on my way. Listen, the global positioning system on my phone works. Santoni knows where I was when I received both calls. You have to leave immediately."

"But—"

"Find a safe place where you'll be surrounded by people. Wal-Mart. Just get the hell out and turn on your damn cell phone for once," he added.

Jamie slammed down the phone. "Come on, Fleas!" she cried. "Let's go." She reached for her purse and fumbled through it for Dave's keys. They weren't there. She checked the counter. Holy crap, they were nowhere to be found. She upended her purse on the kitchen table and raked through the mess, her hands shaking so badly they were almost of no use. Oh, if only she would take five minutes out of her life to straighten her purse. She stuffed everything back in.

Where could she have left them? She looked beneath a stack of newspapers, behind an artificial plant. She stepped on Fleas's paw, and he let out a yelp.

"I'm sorry!" she cried. "Where did I put the damn keys? Where is my cell phone?" The dog took a step back as though he feared he'd done something wrong. "I'm sorry, boy," she said, patting his bony head. "I'm not mad at you,

I'm just losing my mind." She checked her bedroom and came out empty-handed. "I don't believe this," she said, feeling as though she had literally lost her mind.

OK, think, she told herself. Maybe she'd accidentally left them in Dave's truck. Or maybe they'd fallen out of her purse on the way in. Anything was possible in her current state of mind.

She raced to the door and jerked it open.

Michael Juliano was standing on the other side.

MAX PULLED INTO THE PARKING LOT OF A convenience store. He punched several buttons on his phone.

"Why are we stopping?" Muffin asked.

"I have to disable the GPS on this phone. I don't want Santoni looking over my shoulder. Besides, I don't know which way to go," he said. "I don't want to end up driving away from Dave. I have to think."

"OK, back to dead things," Muffin said. "It could mean anything. We automatically think it's the end of a life. Dead people, dead animals."

"It could be an inanimate object," Max said.

"Something that is of no use anymore. A dead cigarette butt, for example. Or old newspapers or trash. Dave could be lying in a landfill or recycling area."

"There's a landfill on the edge of town, also has bins for recyclables on the premises," Muffin said. "I can get you the address, but I can't give you directions because, well, because I'm not equipped for it in this rust bucket."

"I'll check inside." Max got out of the truck and hurried into the convenience store.

"I got the directions," Max said when he returned, "but I have a funny feeling about this. Know what I think?"

"It's too easy. You're being set up."

"Right. I drive up to the landfill, it's dark and probably deserted, and Santoni or one of his thugs will be waiting for me. I'm a perfect target. That's not where Dave is being held."

"Where then?"

"I want you to check all listings under Marconi. Maybe something is in his name."

"I've already done that, remember? All I found was a few bars in Knoxville."

"OK, try the other guy's name. Bennetti," he added. "He may have disappeared, but it wouldn't surprise me if Santoni was using his name. He seems to do that a lot."

"OK, checking," Muffin said. She was back in a matter of seconds. "Uh-oh. You're not going to like it."

"Tell me anyway."

"I typed in the name Bennetti, but nothing came up. Then I typed in the first three letters of Bennetti's name and it pulled up several Bennetts. I acted on a hunch—"

"Computers don't have hunches, Muffin, remember?"

"And I did a crosscheck on Bennett's home number. Not only did I get the number for the landfill, I got several business numbers, including the number for a place called Last Chance Auto Salvage and—"

Max went perfectly still. "Bennett Electric."

"Right. Tom Bennett owns all three. Peter Thomas Bennetti is Tom Bennett, your current employer."

Max sat there for a moment, his jaw working. "That means Santoni knew Dave and I were planning to tap into Rawlins's phone line because Bennett would have told him. Santoni also knew exactly when we tapped into his phone line.

"Santoni has been playing me all along. He put everything into motion before I left Beaumont. He even had time to falsify records so that it looked like Tom Bennett was ripe for acquisition." Max stared out the window. "Jesus Christ, I'm not believing this. How did he move so quickly? How could he have set me up in that length of time?"

"He's good, Max. Damn good."

"I don't get it," Max said. "Why didn't someone just kill Dave and me while we were out there tapping into Santoni's line? Instead, they waited."

"I'm stumped, Max. Santoni is playing a game, and he's not letting anyone in on the rules."

Max sighed. "Damn, I'm going to have to go back in that store and ask for directions."

"It's called Last Chance Auto Salvage," Muffin said as though reading his mind.

Max opened the car door, then paused. "If you think about it, a car that no longer works is as good as dead."

"Max, you don't want to know what I'm thinking. If Last Chance Auto Salvage has a crusher—"

"It's the perfect way to dispose of a body," Max said.

JAMIE BLINKED AT THE MAN WHO CALLED himself Michael Juliano. It was as though a veil had been lifted from her eyes. She had been looking for a mobster, a thug, but Nick Santoni had come in a handsome package and was as polished and persuasive as a politician.

He held up her wallet. "It must've fallen from your purse. I tried to follow you, but I got lost on these damn mountain roads. I was about to give up before I spotted this road. I took a chance and drove down despite all the *No Trespassing* signs. Good thing I did, because I spotted that truck immediately."

Jamie took the wallet but didn't say anything. How had he managed to slip it from her purse without her noticing?

"Are you OK?" he asked. "You look upset." He frowned. "You're not having trouble with your husband, are you?"

Jamie made a split-second decision to play along. "It's a long story, Michael. Listen, I was just on my way out." But he already knew that, she reminded herself. He would suspect that Max had called and told her to get out. The only thing he didn't seem to know at the minute was that she did know his true identity.

"At this hour?" He looked surprised.

"Yes. I need to go to the, um, store. For coffee," she added quickly. "I can't stand to wake up and not have coffee in the house." She realized she was talking too fast, probably not making any sense.

"Why don't I take you? I don't like the idea of your driving on these roads at night, and it's foggy out."

"No, no, I'll be fine," she said, hurrying toward Dave's truck. She noticed the fog. It had come in quickly. "Besides, I might be a while. Sometimes when I can't sleep I drive to Wal-Mart and just spend hours looking around, you know?" She opened the door to the truck. "I seem to have misplaced the keys." She looked, but there was no sight of the keys or her cell phone. She checked the ground.

"What do they look like?" Michael asked.

"They're attached to a leather strip." It suddenly hit her. He hadn't slipped her wallet from her purse. He had taken her wallet, her cell phone, and the keys to Bennett's truck. He had come into the cabin while she was showering. She had not heard the buzzer because of the loud washing machine and because she had been in the bathroom with the water running.

And because she'd been so anxious she had been talking to Fleas nonstop as she had bathed. Or maybe Nick had somehow disabled the alarm.

She turned to Michael. "Listen, I appreciate your dropping off my wallet, but I need to search the cabin for my keys. . . ." She paused as he reached into his pocket and pulled out the leather strip that held both the key to the cabin and the one to Bennett's truck.

Their gazes locked. "Don't make it hard on yourself, Jamie. I don't want to shove you into my car at gunpoint. Just get in."

She stood frozen to her spot. She had not realized Fleas had followed her out, but he nudged her with his wet nose.

"Tell you what. I'll be a nice guy and let you bring the mutt. You know I like him. Shall we?" He put his hand under her elbow and prodded her toward the Jaguar. Jamie did as she was told. He paused long enough to let Fleas get into the back, and then opened the passenger door for Jamie. She hesitated.

"Get in, Jamie."

She got in. She waited until he'd climbed in on the other side before she spoke. "What do you want with me, Nick?" she asked.

He smiled and started the car. "So you've

finally figured it out. I simply want to talk to you, that's all."

"Why can't we talk here?"

"I don't want any interruptions from your boyfriend, Mr. Holt."

"Max is not my boyfriend."

"So you say." He started the car and pulled from the driveway.

Jamie tried to remain calm even as the fear began to build inside her with every heartbeat. "Where are you taking me?"

"Some place where we can talk in private. My home." He hit the automatic lock.

She grimaced in the dark. She was as good as dead.

SIXTEEN

"WHAT HAVE WE GOT?" MUFFIN ASKED ONCE Max had scoped out the property surrounding Last Chance Auto Salvage.

Max began pulling out tools from behind the seat and stuffing them into a backpack. "High-voltage fencing, razor wire, top-of-the line security system, and a badass pit bull."

"Hmm. I didn't realize it was so difficult to find good used automotive parts."

Max slipped on the backpack. "Yeah, well, I have a feeling there's a lot more going on in this place than buying and selling auto parts."

"How far away did you park?" Muffin asked.

"Quarter of a mile. Hard to see clearly because of the fog. I don't think anyone is home, but I don't want to risk Nick or his buddies seeing the truck."

"I can probably take care of the dog."

"Probably?" Max said. "You don't sound too certain, and this dog looks mean as hell."

"I can produce an ultrasonic sound of up to two miles, Max, but you realize I'm only going to be able to distract the animal for a matter of minutes. Once he gets accustomed to the sound he'll go after you. I hope you have pepper spray."

"Yeah."

"You'll have to radio me when you're going in and out. I'll hit him with everything I've got, but I can't make any promises."

"I'll be in touch." Max turned on his flashlight and took off on foot. The light seemed to make the fog worse instead of better. The dog was waiting for him when he arrived back at the salvage yard. He barked and snarled as Max donned thick rubber gloves and cut the fence with special wire cutters that would prevent him from suffering a bad shock.

He picked up his cell phone, punched a button, and radioed Muffin. "I'm ready to go in."

"Are you familiar with the security system?"

"Yeah. It's above standard but nothing I can't handle."

"You may not have more than two or three minutes, Max. Here we go."

Max knew the minute Muffin turned on the high-frequency noise-producing sound, not because he heard it but because the dog suddenly reared his head back and shook it hard. Max peeled back a portion of the fence as the dog seemed to forget everything else for the moment except the noise. He yelped and raced away.

Max very carefully slipped past the fence and ran toward the building. He pulled off one glove, reaching into his shirt pocket where he'd tucked a thin but high-powered flashlight. He held it between his teeth and opened the box. Grabbing a screwdriver from his pocket, he shut down the alarm system within seconds.

"I'm in," Max said, once he'd gone through the heavy metal door.

"I see you haven't lost your touch," Muffin said. "I just turned off the noise."

Max crossed a room with a counter and several hard plastic chairs. "I'm in the reception area." He continued down a hall, past a small kitchen, toward the back of the building. He stopped short when he spied a crisscross of blue lights in front of a set of heavy metal doors.

"Aw, shit!"

"What is it?" Muffin asked.

"Lasers."

"You know what that means," Muffin said.

"Yeah. I'm in the right place."

JAMIE WAS QUIET AS NICK TURNED ON YET another mountain road that seemed to lead farther away from civilization. The fog had worsened, making the ride hazardous, but Nick didn't seem to notice. Jamie gripped the armrest with each twist and turn. Anxiety gnawed at her stomach as she wondered what his plans were.

"You're awfully quiet, Jamie."

"Sorry if I don't feel like playing twenty questions, but my mind is preoccupied."

He chuckled softly. "I know the feeling. I haven't been able to sleep lately. Can't seem to shut off my brain. Have you ever felt like time was running out?"

What a question, she thought. She eyed the locked door. "I think I can relate."

He reached over and took her hand. "I'm sorry if I've frightened you. All I want is for us to talk." He slowed the car and pulled up to a wrought-iron gate. Attached to it was a massive brick wall that Jamie had seen in a photo only hours before.

Nick pushed a button, and his window whispered down. He spoke into a tiny speaker, and the gate immediately slid open. He drove through it, and Jamie watched it close behind them.

"Now, how about that cup of coffee?" Nick said once he'd cut the engine and parked.

Jamie merely shrugged. She remained quiet as he helped her from the car and opened the back door for Fleas. The dog jumped out and shook hard, his ears flapping back and forth.

Jamie glanced around as if impressed by what she saw beneath the tall lighted poles when what she was looking for was an escape route. She noted the outbuildings, heard dogs barking in the distance. The place was probably heavily guarded. She suspected the brick wall encompassed the entire area.

There was no way out.

A man dressed in black emerged from the shadows, two Doberman pinschers beside him, each straining on the leash. Jamie jumped. She recognized him immediately, the man who'd caught her writing down his license tag number, the man who'd taken her notepad. That meant he and Nick knew everything she and Max had been able to find out since arriving in Sweet Pea.

Fleas growled. Nick reached for his collar. "Get the dogs out of here, Rudy."

The man gave Jamie a slow easy smile and walked away, disappearing once more into the dark.

Nick continued holding Fleas's collar. "It's OK, boy," he said. "Don't worry about the dogs, Jamie. I have to keep them on the property due to prowlers."

Yeah, right, she thought.

Together they managed to get Fleas inside the cabin. Jamie was surprised at the dog's aggressiveness; he obviously sensed something wasn't right. She kept petting him, offering him reassurance.

The cabin was spacious and definitely masculine. There wasn't a woman's touch anywhere, not even in the fully equipped kitchen, with its black lacquered cabinets and stainless-steel appliances. A red, black, and yellow abstract painting gave off the only color in the room.

If she lived she would be able to tell her friends she had gotten to see the inside of a killer's house.

Nick walked to the refrigerator. "I offered you coffee, but I have wine if you prefer it."

She didn't need to get drunk; she needed to

get out. "Actually, a glass of water would be fine."

"Certainly." He grabbed two glasses from one of the cabinets and filled them from the refrigerator dispenser. He handed her one of the glasses before reaching for a box of dog biscuits. He offered it to Fleas, but the dog backed away. "Suit yourself, boy."

"He was obviously spooked by your dogs," Jamie said, thinking Fleas was probably smarter than her for not accepting from a man like Nick anything that would be ingested. "He'll be OK in a minute or two."

"Let's sit in the living room."

Like she had a choice. Jamie took the glass and followed him once more, the hound on her heels. She sat down on the leather sofa and was surprised when Nick took the chair next to it instead of sitting beside her.

He looked at her. "You're surprised I'm not already all over you, aren't you, Jamie?" he asked as though reading her mind.

"Well, I—"

"That's why you've felt safe with me all this time. I'm different from most men because I don't try to paw you and get you into my bed. I'm certain a woman with your looks is accustomed to men making unwanted advances."

Jamie remained quiet and took a sip of her water. She would not let him know how nervous she was.

"It's because I respect you. You're different from other women. I'm sorry I had to lie to you in order to make your acquaintance, but there was no other way." He paused. "But then, you lied to me as well. You were willing to use a man you thought had just lost his sister in order to get information from him."

"You said you wanted to talk."

"I want you to know the truth about me, Jamie. I want you to know who and what I am. I'm hoping you'll somehow find a way to understand."

Jamie set her glass down on the table. "I'm supposed to understand what you do for a living, Nick?" she said in disbelief. "Are you serious?"

"If I did half of what I was reputed to have done I wouldn't have time to sleep."

"Did you kill Dave Anderson?"

"Absolutely not. I've never even met the man. He was trespassing on my property, and one of the dogs bit him."

"What about Harlan?"

He shook his head, a sad smile touching his lips. "I don't know why people assume I killed him. I can assure you I did not. Harlan and I were business associates, and we had a very lucrative working relationship."

"You were blackmailing him, extorting money."

"On the contrary, I was protecting him."

"From whom?"

Nick chuckled. "Mostly from himself, dear. Harlan Rawlins had an appetite for women, and he was known to get carried away."

"Did he hurt someone?"

"Even men of God make mistakes. And, yes, he did hurt a woman. Very badly, I might add. He called me in the middle of the night, and I took care of it."

"How?"

"I saw to it the woman had immediate medical attention, that she was paid very well for her, um, trouble, and that Harlan's name never came up."

"Why would you protect a man like that?"

Nick arched one brow. "Why?" He stood. "Jamie, I'm a businessman and a realist. Harlan was a human being like the rest of us. He used poor judgment. But look at what he accomplished. I am the one who insisted he hire a bodyguard, not only out of concern for crazy religious fanatics who might take offense over his teachings but to make certain Harlan remained stable. The man had a lot of emotional problems, Jamie. And I supplied more protection by having security personnel travel with the ministry. Harlan never had to worry about someone torching one of his tents. I even hired his administrative assistant and public relations person to give Harlan a little more polish. He was just a country preacher before I took over. I made him a star in just a few years. Was I wrong to collect a salary?"

Jamie didn't know how to respond. Nick Santoni had just painted a very appealing picture of himself. "Did you hire a hit man to take out Max?"

Nick laughed out loud. Jamie shot him a dark look. "I'm sorry, Jamie, but if you knew how that sounded. People like me don't hire hit men, they hire good attorneys."

"What do you mean?"

"Meaning, Harlan and I put together a large and legitimate bid on Max Holt's TV network, but it was ignored, and their dealings with me weren't fair or legal. I was planning to sue Max. Why would I pay someone to kill a man when I can take that man to court and win a considerable amount of money?"

He was good, Jamie thought, but then Nick

Santoni had obviously practiced. "Who do you think killed Harlan?"

"I think his wife did it. Harlan was cruel to her."

"What do you want with me, Nick?"

"I like you, Jamie. I'd like for us to have the opportunity to get to know one another. I'm leaving Sweet Pea in a matter of hours. I've chartered a plane, and I want you on it with me."

"Am I being held against my will?"

He looked amused. "That wall is there to keep people out, not in. You are free to walk out that door anytime you like. At the same time, you must realize you're at risk."

"What do you mean?"

"The police are looking for Harlan's killer. You were the last person to see him alive. I can protect you should the police somehow learn of your visit, should they find out who and where you are." He paused. "I can give you the kind of life you've never dreamed of."

Jamie just stared at him. Why did he want her with him? He wasn't in love with her. He hadn't had time to fall in love with her.

"Jamie?"

She looked at him. "I can't do that, Nick."

His jaw stiffened, and his eyes became dark.

"Because of Holt?" he asked, his words clipped and precise.

Jamie saw the change come over him. It had been so subtle in the car, but the Nick Santoni she was looking at now was the man Max had tried to warn her about.

"It's a known fact, Jamie: You're Max Holt's girl."

"His girl?"

"His woman. But I want you. I can offer you the kind of life you always wanted."

Jamie stared openly.

"I have made it my business to find out about you. I know what you desire the most," he added in the gentlest of voices. "I will make all your dreams come true, Jamie."

Jamie was almost in awe. Nick Santoni was good. Damn good. He knew how to draw people in, seduce them, practically hypnotize them. She could see how many women could be lured in by him.

"You don't have to carry the world on your shoulders anymore, Jamie. I'll be there."

"What about Max?"

"You hold his life in your hands. If you go with me, I will see that nothing happens to him. If you don't, all bets are off."

MAX STUDIED THE WIRES CAREFULLY. SAN-
toni had spent a ton of money on his inside
security system, and although it was state-of-
the-art and the best available on the current
market, Max knew the system well because
he'd used it as a baseline to design his own.
The only difference, Max's design would not
be available to the consumer for another couple
of years. He did not feel at all guilty when he
was able to disarm Nick's in less than a minute. The blue laser lights disappeared, and Max
pushed through the double doors. He passed
through an office with several computers. He'd
definitely want to take a look at them, but he
had other things on his mind, including finding
Dave Anderson. Max walked into the next
room, flipped on a light switch, and gave a low
whistle when he found himself staring at an
entire arsenal of weapons.

"Well, well," he said.

"What's going on, Max?" Muffin asked.

"I found Santoni's playroom." Max looked
about the room. He spied a wooden box the
size of a coffin. Taking a deep breath, he
walked over to it and carefully lifted the lid.

Dave Anderson lay inside, wrists and ankles tied together. He opened his eyes.

"I'm dying, Max. They put me in here so I could bleed to death. I'm pretty sure the dog hit a major artery, because I can feel my life-blood draining from me."

"Where did the dog bite you?"

"Inside my right thigh. Nick's thug called him off because he obviously didn't want to kill me right away. He wanted me to die slowly. I'm surprised I'm still alive."

Max saw blood on Dave's pants. "Lay still, Dave." He pulled out a pocketknife and made a slit in Dave's slacks. He pulled back the material. "It's a nasty bite," he said. "You need medical attention, but you're not likely to die."

"You're just saying that."

"I'm telling you the truth."

Max punched a button on his cell phone. "Muffin, I found Dave. I need to get him to the hospital."

"I'm going to lose my leg, aren't I?" Dave said.

"You're not going to lose your leg, for Pete's sake," Max said. "Now be still so I can cut your bindings." He sawed through them with his knife and pulled Dave up so the man was sitting.

"I'm light-headed from losing half my blood," Dave said.

"Do you think you can walk?"

"*Walk?*" he repeated as if the thought were merely ludicrous. "Are you kidding?"

"I'll help you," Max said. "Muffin, can you get us out of here?"

"I can try," she said.

JAMIE SAT ON THE BED IN NICK'S GUEST ROOM and pondered her next move. She'd been sent there to rest. And to make up her mind as to what she was going to do with regard to Nick's invitation to leave with him.

Invitation, her foot!

Fleas had his head propped on her knees. She could tell he was as anxious as she was. And she had thought him dumb. She leaned over and pressed her cheek against the top of his head.

"If only I could talk to Max," she whispered so softly that it was little more than a thought. She glanced around. It did not surprise her to find there was no telephone in the room. She desperately needed to talk to Max, warn him. Although Nick had promised no harm would come to Max, she knew Nick's men would shoot him if he came near the property.

Jamie realized she wasn't thinking straight. She had not slept in hours. She felt wired. Too much had happened in such a short period of time; her mind and body were still trying to adjust. "Lie down, boy," she told Fleas. He did as he was told, propping his head on his paws. He looked sad.

Jamie suddenly realized she was shivering. She hadn't quite grown accustomed to the cool mountain nights, and Nick obviously kept the air-conditioning low. She noted the quilt on a nearby chair and draped it across her shoulders. Her eyes burned. Finally, unable to fight the exhaustion, she curled up on the bed. Fleas scooted closer, as if he felt by doing so he could protect her. Jamie stroked his ear. If only she could close her eyes for five minutes. Just five minutes.

MAX PULLED UP TO THE EMERGENCY EN-trance. "Stay put," he told Dave. "I'm going to get a wheelchair."

"Just ask for a body bag," Dave said.

Max ignored him and climbed from the car. He hurried inside.

"Oh, damn," Dave muttered.

"What is it *now*?" Muffin asked.

"I hope they take me right in. I don't like being around sick people. All those germs."

"You know what I don't understand?" Muffin said. "I don't understand why Max puts up with you. You're the biggest pain in the ass I've ever met. Now why don't you stop sniveling and cut us all a little slack?"

Max and an orderly were back in a matter of minutes. Max opened the passenger door. "Dave, this is Carter. He's going to help you inside, and the doctor is going to take you right in."

"Thank God. Where are you going?"

"I need to call Jamie."

Dave nodded and allowed them to help him into the wheelchair. "Don't worry about me, Max," he said, offering a tight smile. "I'll be all right. Just make sure Jamie's OK."

Max arched one brow but climbed into his car. Muffin was waiting.

"I've already tried Jamie twice," she said. "She's not answering her cell phone."

"Dammit," Max said. "She probably forgot to turn it on again."

"You probably scared the crap out of her when you called and told her to leave the cabin."

"OK, try paging her at Wal-Mart." He chuckled. "If she doesn't answer, tell them to try the menswear section. She might be looking for a new victim."

"I'm going to pretend you didn't say that."

Max waited.

"She didn't respond to the page," Muffin said when she came back on. "They paged her twice. I told them it was an emergency, so they're still trying. I'm on hold."

Max rubbed his hand across his forehead. "Answer the page, Jamie," he muttered under his breath.

"Still nothing," Muffin said.

He sighed. "Tell me this isn't happening."

Max drove on. "Damned if it's not one thing after another." He waited. "Muffin?"

"She's not in the store, Max."

"Shit! Where would she be at this hour of the morning?"

"Maybe she met her friend Michael. I know she likes talking to him."

Max pondered it. "I can't believe she'd go off with him at this hour."

"Maybe Jamie was afraid to be alone."

He was silent for a moment. "What do you know about this guy? This Michael?"

"They met at Wal-Mart, had breakfast a couple of times, and then went to dinner. I know he drives a Jaguar because Jamie said it was really nice."

"Wonder where they went for breakfast?"

"I don't know the name of it, but it's not far from Wal-Mart."

"Shit." Max pulled from the hospital parking lot. He made good time for a truck that was on its last legs. He drove until he spotted the Wal-Mart store. At the light he took a right. He pulled into the first restaurant he saw. "Wish me luck," he told Muffin as he climbed from the truck.

A blast of cold air hit him as he stepped inside the restaurant. The lights were blinding, and the place smelled of coffee and bacon grease. A tired-looking waitress handed him a menu.

"Long night?" he asked her.

"Yeah. I'm filling in for somebody. Not used to these late hours. You want coffee?"

"Please."

She returned a moment later with a steaming mug and set it before him. "What'll it be?"

"This is fine."

"You're either out late or up early," she said.

"A little of both, I guess," Max told her. "Actually, I'm looking for somebody."

"Yeah?"

"I'll bet you could help me. I'll bet you

know most of the customers who come in here."

She shrugged. "I work the breakfast and lunch shift."

"I'm curious about a guy named Michael. He drives a Jaguar. You know him?"

"Depends on who's asking and why."

Max raised his hand, exposing a $100 bill. "I think he's seeing my girlfriend. It's over between us, but I'd like to know. Pride and all that."

"Pretty blonde?"

"Yep."

The waitress reached for the money. "Sorry, I don't get involved in Mr. Juliano's personal affairs." She walked away.

Max sat there for a moment, his expression frozen in place. He stood slowly and made for the door. Muffin was waiting when he climbed inside the truck.

"That was quick. What'd you find out?"

Max opened his mouth to speak, but the words didn't come. He cleared his throat. "It's bad," he whispered.

"Max? What is it?"

"I know why Nick Santoni has been playing games with us. He wanted Jamie."

"Max, what are you talking about?"

"Nick Santoni has Jamie."

SEVENTEEN

Jamie opened her eyes and discovered she'd slept almost three hours. She bolted upright, blinked several times, tried to clear her head. She got up and walked into the adjoining bathroom. She almost didn't recognize the woman in the mirror. Fatigue had painted dark shadows beneath her eyes, and she looked pale.

"If I live through this I'm going to have to start taking better care of myself," she muttered.

She turned on the cold water and splashed it on her face, but when she reached for a towel, she found none. Her face dripping, she opened the drawer beside the sink. It contained unopened bottles of shampoos, lotions, soaps, and toothbrushes. For overnight guests, she thought. Odd that a man like Nick Santoni would think of something like that. No, it probably was the work of a housekeeper.

Jamie opened the cabinet door and reached for a towel. Beneath the stack she saw a slender white telephone. She pulled it out, not at all surprised to find it there.

Nick had known she would find it. He knew she would try to contact Max. Whether he knew she would have suspected as much she could only guess. The only thing Jamie knew for certain was that she had to protect Max at any cost.

Any cost.

The phone jack was easy to find. Jamie plugged in the telephone and dialed Max's cell number. He answered on the first ring.

"It's me," she said.

"Jesus Christ, Jamie, where are you?"

Had Jamie not been listening for the soft click on her end, she would not have heard it. Nor did she miss the relief in Max's voice. "I can't give you that information, Max. I only have a second to talk."

"Jamie, listen to me. Michael Juliano is Nick Santoni."

"I know."

"Is he there?"

"Not at the moment. Max, I've decided to go away with Nick. He wants to make a fresh start."

Silence. Finally, he spoke. "I see."

"I knew you would."

"Are you sure about this, Jamie? Do you know what you're getting into?"

"Nick wants to make a fresh start."

"So what the hell do you want from me?" Max's voice was terse.

"I'm asking you to back off. Give Nick and me this chance."

"You want me to just forget everything, walk away, and let you screw up your life? The man almost killed us. Dammit, Jamie, I thought you were smarter than this."

"I'm not screwing up my life, and even if I were, it's none of your business."

"What about us?"

"There is no us, Max. How many times have I told you? Back off." Jamie hung up the telephone and returned it to Nick's hiding place. She was pretty certain Max was with the program; he was good at reading between the lines.

Someone knocked at the door. She stood and crossed the room. She found one of Santoni's men holding a tray of food and a small pot of coffee.

"Mr. Santoni thought you might want a snack."

Jamie stepped back, and he carried the tray inside and placed it on a round table beside the chair. "Thank you," she said. "Is the fog lifting?"

He did little more than look her way. "Mr. Santoni will be in shortly," was all he said before he closed the door behind him.

Jamie ignored the small wedge of Brie and fruit and delicate finger sandwiches, instead reaching for the silver coffee server. The china was delicate—white, edged with gold. A linen napkin with Nick's initials covered a small basket of croissants with various jams and jellies.

Fleas thumped his tail, an expectant look on his face.

"OK, come here." Jamie fed him three finger sandwiches before she turned to her coffee. She barely had time to finish her cup before someone knocked. "Come in."

Nick Santoni stepped in and closed the door behind him. Fleas walked closer to Jamie and propped his chin on her lap. Nick chuckled. "I'm glad you were able to rest." He glanced at the tray. "Did you eat or did you feed it to the dog?"

"I could use a cigarette," Jamie said, ignoring his question.

Nick pulled open the drawer in the bedside table and produced her brand of cigarettes, a gold lighter, and a crystal ashtray, which he set on the table. He opened the cigarette pack, offered her one, and lit it for her. Fleas's eyes followed his every move.

"It's OK, boy," Nick said, although he didn't reach out and pet Fleas as he usually did.

"You obviously planned for my visit," Jamie said, inhaling the smoke. It burned her lungs, and she realized she was going to have to either get used to smoking again or give it up altogether. Neither sounded particularly appealing at the moment.

Nick sat on the edge of the bed. "Yes. And for longer than you think. At first all I could think of was getting even with Holt. Until I found out about you." He glanced at the pack of cigarettes. "I know you sometimes smoke when you're upset, although you gave it up some time ago."

"You know a lot about me, Nick."

"Yes."

"Why did you check me out?"

"I was curious. I figured you must be pretty special to capture Maximillian Holt's attention."

"I'm hardly the first woman Max has taken a second look at."

"True. But you've certainly managed to hold his interest, haven't you?"

Jamie met his gaze, a question in her eyes. "You find me appealing because Max likes me?"

He smiled. "Perhaps in the beginning. Now that I know you personally I can't help but like you."

Jamie watched as he reached for the coffee server, refilled her cup, and added the amount of cream and sugar she liked. Then, with hands that appeared too large to grip the dainty handle, he offered it to her.

She sipped as he watched.

"I need to know your decision," he said quietly.

She returned the cup to its saucer. "I'm coming with you."

"Do I sense regret in your voice?"

Jamie could feel his eyes boring into her. She raised her head and met his gaze. "Don't push it, Nick."

He stood. "We leave at dawn. The fog should have lifted by then."

"WHAT DO YOU THINK?" MUFFIN ASKED MAX.

"I think Nick knows his eggs are fried, as Jamie would say."

"Could you put that into words that a brilliant computer like me can understand?"

"His time is up. He's planning to leave the country. He'll probably use the local airstrip to get out of Sweet Pea."

"I just heard back from Jersey. Leo Santoni was one pissed mother when I woke him."

"Not my problem. What'd he say?"

"He'll cooperate."

Max nodded. "I guess we're going to have to call in the big guns. Call Quantico and find out where Helms is. Tell him I'll need backup. He'll probably have to send someone local. Also, tell him if he wants Santoni, we play by my rules."

"You're such a hard-ass."

"Where Jamie's life is concerned you're damn right."

RUDY MARCONI WAS WAITING FOR NICK when the man stepped out of the bedroom.

They didn't speak until they were inside Nick's office on the other side of the house.

"We couldn't trace the call," Rudy said, "and Holt hasn't returned to the cabin. We've got the place surrounded, but there has been no sign of him."

Nick began packing his briefcase. "I want him found, Rudy."

"I've never let you down before."

Nick regarded him. "Don't let this be the first. I won't rest until Holt is dead." He closed the briefcase. "Oh, that damn bloodhound has to go, too."

Two hours later Jamie followed Nick outside and into a waiting Hummer. The man called Rudy loaded Fleas and several pieces of luggage into the back.

"Good thing I'm traveling light," Jamie muttered, noting her dog barely had room to move around.

Nick chuckled. "You'll have plenty of time for shopping later."

Rudy and a man named Victor whom Jamie had seen scouring the premises climbed into the front seat. Nick opened the door to the backseat so Jamie could get in. He slid in beside her. They pulled up to the gate, Rudy said a few words, and it slid open for them.

"It'll take us about thirty minutes to reach the landing strip," Rudy said.

"Sounds good." Nick put his hand on Jamie's lap. She didn't move it. Fleas propped his head on her shoulder as though offering support. He obviously sensed a problem; he hadn't left her side all night. "You OK, boy?"

He nudged her chin in response.

"Lie down," Jamie said, not wanting the dog to do anything that might annoy Nick. Fleas sank to the floor.

"He seems agitated," Nick said, patting Jamie's knee. "I wonder if he misses the truck?"

"I think it has more to do with the big guns your boys are carrying."

Nick didn't reply.

Jamie saw they were going down the mountain. They had almost reached the foothills when they came upon a number of cars stopped in front of them. Ahead they saw blue lights flashing.

Nick frowned. "What's going on up there?"

"Looks like some kind of accident," Rudy said.

Victor opened his door. "I'll check it out." He climbed out and hurried down the road.

"Where are we going?" Jamie asked.

"To an airstrip."

"And after that?"

Nick smiled. "It's a surprise. You'll love it."

Jamie thought of her newspaper and the little town in which she'd been born and raised. She wondered if she would ever see Vera again. "Will I be able to write to my friends?" she asked.

"Darling, we will make new friends. You'll be so busy you won't have time to think of your old ones."

"Really?" she said, trying not to sound sarcastic. "Well, you just saved me a shit load of money on Christmas cards and postage."

Victor returned. "It's bad, Boss. Three cars involved, several people hurt. The cops are waiting for an ambulance."

"Did they give any indication how long it would take?"

"Said they were trying to hurry things along, but there's glass everywhere."

Nick leaned his head against the seat. "Call the pilot and inform him we're going to be late."

In the distance, Jamie could hear the wail of a siren. She leaned against the door and closed her eyes, but her thoughts never stilled. Her door was locked. She assumed there was a master lock by the driver's side, which meant she was not going to be able to unlock her door on her own. Nevertheless, as the siren grew louder, Jamie began to hope.

The ambulance arrived, and the siren died. Victor opened his door and headed toward the scene once more. He returned a few minutes later. "They're loading people into the ambulance now. Shouldn't take much longer."

Jamie's heart pounded loudly in her chest as the sirens whined out once more. The ambulance was obviously rushing its victims to the hospital. The car inched its way closer to the scene. When they were less than 100 feet away, Jamie sighed expansively.

"Are you OK?" Nick asked as though sensing a shift in her mood.

"I'm wondering if we're going to sit here forever, that's all."

Nick smiled. "You're an impatient woman."

"Would somebody turn on the radio?"

Rudy glanced over his shoulder at Nick, who nodded his OK.

"See if you can find a good country-western station," Jamie said.

Nick looked surprised. "I would never have suspected you liked that kind of music."

"Yes sir," Jamie said. "I like it fast and loud."

Nick chuckled as a Patsy Cline song came on. Fleas stood in the back and let out a growl.

"Turn it up," Jamie said.

Rudy shrugged and turned it up.

Fleas began to bark.

Nick turned. "What's wrong with him?"

"Maybe he has to go to the bathroom," Jamie said.

"Bad timing, boy," Nick replied.

Fleas became more agitated. He tried to climb over the seat toward Jamie.

"Down, boy!" Nick shouted. The dog snapped at him. "What the hell?"

"He's nervous," Jamie said. "The music will calm him down. Turn it louder."

Rudy did as he was told, and the car was suddenly flooded with loud music.

Fleas snarled and bit Nick. Suddenly the dog was all over him. "Let me out of the damn car!" Nick shouted.

Rudy instantly hit the automatic lock. Jamie opened her door, whistled for Fleas, and ran as fast as she could toward the sheriff's cars. She heard Nick shout her name, but she kept running.

One of the deputies looked up and frowned

at the sight of her. His name tag read: *Higgins.*
"What's wrong, miss?"

"Listen to me!" Jamie cried. "My name is
Jane, and I'm wanted by the police for killing
Harlan Rawlins."

He frowned. "What?"

"I'm Jane!" Jamie cried. "You've seen me
on the news. I killed Harlan Rawlins. I'm
pretty sure there's a reward for my capture.
Something like one hundred grand."

The deputy frowned. "I haven't heard of any
reward. Lady, are you crazy?"

Jamie was only vaguely aware that Nick had
walked up beside her. He suddenly, and without warning, burst into laughter. "Honey, that
is *not* funny."

The deputy looked surprised to see Nick. He
glanced around, then stepped closer. "I didn't
see your car back there, Mr., um, Juliano," he
whispered. "Is everything OK?"

"Fine, Bill. I'm afraid my girlfriend has had
too much to drink. How much longer are we
going to have to wait? We have a plane to
catch."

"I'll clear the way immediately."

Jamie gaped at the man.

"Your hand is bleeding, Nick," Rudy said
once Nick and Jamie were inside the car.

"It's nothing. Just give me something to wrap around it."

Victor passed him a clean handkerchief.

"What do you want me to do with the dog?" Rudy asked.

"Kill him." Nick looked at Jamie. "Use the same knife you used on Rawlins."

DETECTIVE PETE SILLS REACHED FOR THE telephone and mumbled into it. He looked at the clock on his nightstand. Six-thirty in the morning.

"Detective Sills, my name is Helms, and I'm with the FBI. Could you spare me a few minutes of your time? It has to do with the Rawlins case."

Sills sat up and rubbed his eyes. "How can I help you?"

"I think maybe I can help you."

"NO-O-O-O!" JAMIE SCREAMED. SHE LUNGED across Nick's lap and half-fell from the car. Fleas rushed over to her even as Rudy reached for him. "Don't kill him!" Jamie cried, pounding Rudy's thighs with her fists, even as Nick tried to pull her back into the car. "For God's sake, Nick, please don't kill him. Please, oh God, please!" She burst into tears.

"Hold it," Nick said to the man.

Rudy paused, knife in hand.

"The dog is dangerous," Nick told Jamie. "Look what he did to my hand."

Jamie saw the blood soaking into the handkerchief. "It's my fault," she said, sobbing against him. "Fleas goes berserk at the sound of country music. I know it sounds crazy, but it's true. You won't have any more trouble with him. I promise." She looked up. Nick's eyes were hard. "Nick, I swear to God I'll do anything."

Nick didn't seem to be listening.

"If you kill the dog you may as well kill me, because I'm not going to cooperate."

Nick sighed. "The dog comes with us," he said. "Keep the radio off." As Rudy loaded the dog in the back once more, Nick looked at Jamie. "This is your first and last warning: One false move and the dog dies."

SWEET PEA'S AIRPORT WAS NO MORE THAN A length of asphalt beside a small building. A twin-engine aircraft waited, lights flashing on each wing, the stairs lowered and ready for boarding.

The pilot and co-pilot wore crisp uniforms and nodded at the group as they assisted Nick's men in loading the luggage. Nick helped Jamie out of the Hummer as the pilot waited at the bottom of the steps. Fleas sidled up to Jamie.

"Jamie, I'm afraid we can't take the dog," Nick said.

She blinked at him. "You promised."

"It's not really up to me."

"Bullshit. You make all the rules."

"I can't risk taking the animal on board an aircraft. Not after what happened earlier."

"I've already explained—"

"Rudy will see that Fleas has a good home."

"I'm not going without him, Nick."

"Don't be difficult, Jamie. I have enough to worry about at the moment. I'll buy you a new dog when we get to where we're going. You can have as many pets as you like."

"I don't want a new dog."

Rudy stepped up to Nick. "We've got trouble." He nodded toward the road that led to the airport.

Jamie turned in the direction they were staring. She sucked in her breath at the sight of her truck bouncing along the road, Max at the wheel.

Nick looked at Jamie. "How did he find out?"

"You're asking me?"

"You spoke with him earlier."

"And you heard every word of my conversation. I never mentioned we were going to the airport, he figured it out for himself. I think you underestimate Max."

"Get on the plane."

"Not without my dog."

Nick slapped her hard. "Either you get on the plane now or I order Rudy to shoot him."

Jamie tasted blood. "I don't take orders from you!" she shouted. "I'm not one of your *boys*. You shoot my dog and you'd better be prepared to shoot me, because I'm going to do my best to kill you with my bare hands. I will *not* get on that plane without my dog, you got that?"

"What the hell do you want me to do about Holt?" Rudy asked as Max turned onto the road leading to the landing strip.

"Kill him and the dog both."

Jamie almost choked on her anger. She grabbed Nick by the collar. "Leave them out of this, do you hear me? I said I'd cooperate, but you have to keep your part of the bargain. Nick, I'm telling you, you do not want to piss me off."

He almost looked amused. "Are you trying to frighten me, Jamie?"

"No, I'm just telling you what a bitch I can be. You leave my dog behind and you're going to regret the day you climbed in an airplane with me. And from the way you talk, we're going to be in the air a long time. Think about it."

Max parked the truck close by and climbed out. He looked at Jamie, noting the blood on her lip. "You know, Nick, I didn't like you before, but I like you even less now. I don't have much respect for a man who would strike a woman."

"You act as if that matters to me, Mr. Holt," Nick said. "You're as good as dead. Why should your opinion of me matter?"

"You plan to shoot an unarmed man in front of your new girlfriend? She doesn't like you to begin with; why risk alienating her further?"

Nick merely smiled.

"Your egg is fried, Nick."

"Meaning?"

"The jig is up."

"Not exactly." With lightning speed Nick

pulled Jamie against him and put a gun to her head.

Jamie felt as though her heart would literally take flight from her chest. Damn her and her mouth. "Nick, I was sort of exaggerating about how nasty I was going to act on the plane. Why can't we just leave Fleas with Max and get going?"

"She's lying, Nick," Max said. "You don't do things her way and she turns into Satan's daughter."

"You two obviously think this is funny," Nick said. "Max, tell me: How would you like to watch my man Rudy cut Jamie like he did Harlan? Would you find that funny? I think her death would be harder on you than your own."

"Damn," Max said. "You just implicated yourself in Harlan Rawlins's murder."

"We both know he was already dead. The fool was popping pills like they were candy."

"You were his supplier; you knew exactly what you were doing. Some pills just don't mix, and you knew that."

"You're right. Harlan overdosed, but I just wanted to leave my mark on him, and Rudy is so good with a knife."

"I wouldn't pull that trigger if I were you," Max said. He nodded toward the airplane, where an elderly gentleman stood at the door of the craft.

Nick turned and froze. "What the hell?"

The pilot assisted the man down the steps. Once the men had cleared them, the pilot stepped aside and the other man crossed the short distance to where they were standing.

"Hello, Nicholas."

"Uncle Leo, what the hell are you doing here?"

Rudy and his partner lowered their rifles and stepped back.

"I see you've managed to dig your hole deeper. Give me the gun, Nicholas."

He gave a short laugh. "Are you kidding? Do you know who these people are?"

"Yes. And do you know what will happen to the Santoni family if you kill Max Holt and Miss Swift?" He didn't wait for Nick's response. "It's time for you to come home. This is the last time I'm going to ask nicely."

"Are you out of your mind, old man?"

"Give me the gun, Nicky. Don't dishonor me in front of these people."

Nick seemed to ponder it. He started to lower the gun, then jerked it back and aimed it in the direction of his uncle. He pulled the trigger, and the man jerked as the bullet hit him

square in the chest. Jamie screamed as Leo
Santoni fell to the tarmac, but not before she
saw Nick and his men aim their guns in Max's
direction.

"It's your turn, Holt," Nick said. He'd barely
gotten the words out of his mouth before more
shots were fired. Jamie watched in horror as
Nick and Rudy crumpled to the ground. Where
the hell were the shots coming from?

Max reached for her, and the two pilots
cleared the steps, each of them armed. Jamie
went willingly into Max's arms. From the corner of her eye she saw Nick move. He raised
his gun and aimed in her direction. In a split
second Max was in front of her, and Fleas
pounced on Nick. His gun went off, and the
animal howled and went down. Another shot
was fired at Nick's head and he fell back.

Jamie screamed and buried her face against
Max's chest, not wanting to see any more
bloodshed. Finally, she broke free from Max
and ran to her dog. "Fleas, no!" she screamed.
"Please don't die. Please don't die."

Max was beside her in seconds. "He's going
to be OK, Jamie."

"He's not going to make it," she said, chok-
ing back a sob. "He took a bullet for me. He's
going to die out here with a bunch of mob-

sters." She kissed the dog on the top of the head. "He looks so sad, Max. He knows he's dying. I was such a bad master, and he knew it. He probably took the bullet on purpose."

"He always looks sad, Jamie, and he is not likely to die from a wounded tail."

"What?" Jamie looked up.

"The bullet nicked his tail, babe, that's all."

Jamie rose and quickly surveyed the damage. Obviously, a bullet had indeed nicked Fleas's tail about six inches up from the tip. "Is that all? Jeez, there's not even that much blood. Good grief, what a sissy!"

"I'm sure it still hurts like hell," Max said.

As if acting on cue, Fleas moaned.

One of the pilots dropped to his knees beside them. "Are you two OK?"

Max nodded. "Yeah."

"How's the mutt?"

Max chuckled. "I believe he'll live."

"The others are dead. I've already phoned headquarters."

"Who are you?" Jamie blurted.

"Agent Decker with the FBI, ma'am. You sure you're OK?"

"I'm having a nervous breakdown, and I skinned my knee. Other than that—"

"You don't know how long we've waited to

get Santoni off the streets, but he was always one step ahead of us."

Jamie stared at Max. "Why was Leo Santoni on the plane?"

"I called him," Max said. "He was trying to convince Nick to come home before he did more damage to the family. I told him I'd hand over Nick in exchange for our safety. I didn't mention I was contacting the FBI. I feel bad that it ended this way."

"Don't," Agent Decker said. "Leo might look old and frail, but there was a time he was as bad as his nephew." The man glanced at Nick, sprawled on the tarmac. "I don't think he would have fared any better with the Santoni family." He gave a satisfied sigh. "We've already picked up Tom Bennett for questioning; we're going to find out who all was on Santoni's payroll."

Jamie refused to look in the dead men's direction. That didn't mean she was sorry they were dead, though. "There's a sheriff's deputy," Jamie said. "I think he may have been working for Santoni. His name is Bill Higgins."

Decker jotted it down. Finally, he offered Max his hand. "Mr. Holt, you managed to help us get two of the most powerful men in the

Santoni family off the street. Once we seize their property and their computers we'll be able to learn more about the operation."

"You may not be able to break the code," Max said. "I've been trying."

"Helms said we could count on you for assistance."

"Yeah, he would say that. By the way, I have another job for you guys. I want you to pick up the man who heads up my mergers and acquisitions, pronto. I want a full investigation. I strongly suspect he's involved in this somehow."

"Right away, Mr. Holt."

Jamie shot a startled look in Max's direction. "What about Dave? Is he?"

"I spoke with him earlier. They stitched him up; he's fine."

Fleas, obviously having come to the conclusion he was no longer the center of attention, stood and shook, his big ears flapping in the light breeze. Finally, he sat down and started licking his wounded tail. As though discovering it wasn't as bad as he'd thought, he began licking his privates.

Jamie grimaced. "I *hate* when he does that!"

Decker patted the dog on the head. "Headquarters is sending people right away, Mr.

Holt. In five minutes this place will be crawling with cops, probably a couple of local reporters. It would be best if you and Miss Swift weren't here when they arrived."

Jamie looked at Max.

He met her gaze. "You know how I hate publicity."

"What about my story?"

"Jamie, we have to talk."

"No, Max, I'm not going to back down this time. I specifically came here for my story." Then she remembered Rudy had taken her notepad. "Oh, damn."

"What is it?" Max asked. "Lost your notes?"

EPILOGUE

Max began at the nape of her neck, nuzzling the little indentation at the top of her spine, then running his tongue downward, touching each vertebra as he went. Jamie shivered and buried her face against the feather pillow. Max's big hands skimmed her hips, slightly rough against her smooth skin. He trailed his fingers down one thigh, behind one knee, down her calf.

Finally, he coaxed her onto her back.

And studied her.

Her face was lovely, her cheeks heightened a dusty rose that hinted at her own arousal. Her blonde hair was rich and glowing, the color of ripened wheat, wisps framing her face, loose tendrils brushing against gently sloping shoulders. Her skin seemed to glow.

She was perfect in every way. Each curve, each swell, looked as though a master artist had sculpted it.

Jamie's eyes fluttered open as Max scooted upward on the bed and covered her mouth with his. It was the kind of kiss that women only dreamed of, the kind they could sink their hearts into. Max parted her lips with his tongue and tasted her. Jamie felt a ripple of pleasure as his hand cupped one breast.

Jamie opened her eyes and stared at the ceiling. Morning. She felt the coarse sheet beneath her; the smell of pine trees and a bloodhound that was in dire need of a bath had replaced the scent of lavender. "Aw, shit," she muttered.

At the foot of the bed, Fleas rolled over and looked at her. He had obviously sneaked up on the bed during the night.

"OK," she said, "so I was dreaming about sex again. With Max," she added. "It happens all the time." She sat up, and her hair tumbled into her face. Her sleep shirt was wrinkled, and she needed to find her toothbrush. Why couldn't she be as gorgeous as she was in her dreams?

"Welcome to the real world, Jamie Swift," she muttered.

DAVE DID NOT LOOK HAPPY WHEN MAX AND Jamie entered his hospital room. He was wearing a dark frown and a surgical mask.

"What's wrong?" Max asked.

"What's wrong?" Dave echoed, his voice muffled from the mask. He pulled it down. "I'm in a hospital surrounded by illness and disease and you ask me what's wrong? Not only that, I'm risking my life being here. Do you have any idea the number of people who are killed each year in hospitals simply because a doctor or nurse makes an error? I'd have a better chance on an open battlefield."

"How long are they keeping you?" Jamie asked.

"Another day at least. They're giving me antibiotics to fight off an infection, but they don't think I should be treated for rabies because, well, because—"

"Yeah?" Max said.

"I'm not exhibiting any symptoms." He suddenly laughed. "And believe me, I've checked."

Max and Jamie laughed with him.

"I don't know how you guys managed to put up with me," Dave said, still chuckling. "You probably need a vacation. *I* need a vacation from myself."

"My private plane is at your disposal," Max said. He reached into his pocket for his business card. "I've listed a number on the back. Call this person when you're ready to check out of this hotel." He paused. "I'd like to see you back at work in a couple of weeks."

Dave took the card. He raised his eyes to Max's, and they exchanged smiles. "Hey, man, I'm really glad we got Santoni."

AN HOUR LATER, MAX PULLED INTO THE parking lot of a small Catholic church. "Why are we stopping here?" Jamie asked.

"I have an appointment with a priest. You want to get hitched while we're here?"

Jamie rolled her eyes. "What's this really about?"

"I'll be right back."

Jamie watched him go. "Muffin?"

"I'm here."

"Why is Max meeting with a priest?"

"He's making an anonymous donation to the community. You didn't hear it from me."

Max rejoined Jamie a few minutes later.

"You never fail to amaze me," she said once he'd climbed into the truck and started the engine.

"Oh, yeah?" He looked at her.

"Yeah."

"Does that mean we're going to have hot steamy sex when we get back to the cabin?"

Jamie felt her face grow hot. Well, OK, that wasn't the only body part that warmed at his words. "I, um, well—"

"Easy for you to say," Max teased.

MAX WAS IN THE PROCESS OF PACKING HIS BElongings when Jamie hung up after talking to Vera. She frowned at him.

"What'd I do this time?"

"You bought me a car. A red Mustang," she added. "Vera just told me."

"I felt bad because your other car got shot up by Santoni's hit man. I didn't want you to be without transportation while it's in the shop."

"What am I supposed to do with two cars and a truck? My driveway isn't big enough."

"That truck is on its last legs."

"That truck will be running long after your so-called Maxmobile gives out, Max. Besides,

I have to keep it for Fleas. I'll park it in the backyard and grow flowers around it."

They were interrupted by a knock on the door. "That's probably the guy with the trailer."

"I DON'T BELIEVE THIS," MAX SAID ONCE THEY were on the road. "I have seen a lot of dumb things in my day, but I've never seen anything as dumb as this."

"I agree," Muffin said. "It's pretty dumb."

"It doesn't look that dumb," Jamie muttered, although she was careful to stay low in the seat so those in traffic couldn't see her.

Max glanced her way. "You don't think we look strange driving a worthless pickup truck and pulling a two-million-dollar car?"

"Just so Fleas can ride in the back of the truck with us?" Muffin added. "I hope my laptop friend at MIT doesn't hear about this. I'll never be able to live it down."

"Do you have any better suggestions?" Jamie asked. "We didn't have time to get Muffin reinstalled in your car, which is why you refused to let me go back to Beaumont in my truck."

Max grinned. "That's not the only reason,

Swifty. I knew you couldn't bear the thought of leaving me."

Jamie ignored him, despite the gentle pull in her stomach. Max only had to look at her to send her thoughts into a wild frenzy. She glanced over her shoulder at Fleas, who was sitting on a feather mattress and gnawing on a foot-long rawhide bone. "I think he survived the trauma well."

"What trauma?" Muffin said. "Nothing happened. We weren't involved in finding Santoni, remember? You guys need to read the newspaper. The FBI shot and killed two mob figures at a small airstrip, and, acting on a hunch, they broke into an auto salvage company owned by one Thomas Peter Bennetti, aka Tom Bennett, and found a small arsenal. Not only that, they've managed to break through the firewall on the computer. That part wasn't in the newspaper; I found out on my own. So what it boils down to is once again we solved the case and someone else gets the credit."

Max grunted. "The FBI won't be able to decipher Santoni's codes."

"Oh, listen to Mr. Genius," Muffin said. "He couldn't break the code, so he doesn't think anyone else can."

"I could have broken it if I'd had more

time," Max said. He sighed. "What we need now is a nice vacation. What do you think, Swifty? I've got this nice boat."

Muffin grunted. "It's one hundred and fifty feet long, Max. I believe it's called a yacht."

Max tossed Jamie a lazy smile. "We could just hop on and go, just the two of us and—"

"Along with a crew of about twenty," Muffin interrupted.

"You and me, Swifty. Lots of sun, blue sky, and water."

Jamie peered over him from the top of her sunglasses. "You and me on a yacht in the middle of the ocean? That sounds more dangerous than anything we've been through so far. Bad idea, Max."

He smiled. "Jamie, Jamie, Jamie. We're a long way from home, and I can't drive over forty miles per hour in this heap. I'll have plenty of time to wear you down."